ie blus   ot.
vis liked

moved clos   nst
cab of the truck so that his arms encased
. He looked into her eyes. Looked at her
s. Gave her a second to figure out what was
ming.

Ohmygod, she thought. *Oh—my—God!*

e lifted her off the ground, one arm around
er waist. Her face was on a level with his; he
issed her slowly, caught her lip between his
eth and sucked on her flesh, and—and—

e kissed the place where her neck and shoulder
ined.

was magic.

er eyes closed; the world went away.

d when he asked her to go home with him
gave him the only logical answer—because,
r all, she was nothing if not logical.

e said, "Yes."

THE WILDE BROTHERS

Wilde by name, unashamedly wild by nature!

They work hard, but you can be damned sure they play even harder! For as long as any of them could remember, they've always loved the same things: Danger…and beautiful women.

They gladly took up the call to serve their country, but duty, honour and pride are words that mask the scars of a true warrior. Now, one by one, the brothers return to their family ranch in Texas.

Can their hearts be tamed in the place they once called home?

Meet the deliciously sexy **Wilde Brothers** in this sizzling and utterly unmissable new family dynasty by much-loved author Sandra Marton!

In August you met

THE DANGEROUS JACOB WILDE

In December were you able to resist

THE RUTHLESS CALEB WILDE?

This month meet

THE MERCILESS TRAVIS WILDE

THE MERCILESS TRAVIS WILDE

BY
SANDRA MARTON

First published in Great Britain 2013
by Mills & Boon, an imprint of Harlequin (UK) Limited.
Harlequin (UK) Limited, Eton House, 18-24 Paradise Road,
Richmond, Surrey TW9 1SR

© Sandra Marton 2013

ISBN: 978 0 263 89998 6

Sandra Marton wrote her first novel while she was still in primary school. Her doting parents told her she'd be a writer some day, and Sandra believed them. In secondary school and college she wrote dark poetry nobody but her boyfriend understood—though, looking back, she suspects he was just being kind. As a wife and mother she wrote murky short stories in what little spare time she could manage, but not even her boyfriend-turned-husband could pretend to understand those. Sandra tried her hand at other things, among them teaching and serving on the Board of Education in her home town, but the dream of becoming a writer was always in her heart.

At last Sandra realised she wanted to write books about what all women hope to find: love with that one special man, love that's rich with fire and passion, love that lasts for ever. She wrote a novel, her very first, and sold it to Mills & Boon® Modern™ Romance. Since then she's written more than sixty books, all of them featuring sexy, gorgeous, larger-than-life heroes. A four-time RITA® award finalist, she's also received five *RT Book Reviews* magazine awards, and has been honoured with *RT*'s Career Achievement Award for Series Romance. Sandra lives with her very own sexy, gorgeous, larger-than-life hero in a sun-filled house on a quiet country lane in the north-eastern United States.

Recent titles by the same author:

Did you know these are also available as eBooks?
Visit www.millsandboon.co.uk

CHAPTER ONE

For as long as Travis Wilde could remember, Friday nights had belonged to his brothers and him.

They'd started setting those evenings aside way back in high school. Nobody had made a formal announcement. Nobody had said, "Hey, how about we make Friday evenings ours?"

It had just happened, was all, and over the ensuing years, it had become an unspoken tradition.

The Wildes got together on Fridays, no matter what.

Always.

Okay.

Maybe not always.

One of them might be away on business, Caleb on one coast or the other, dealing with a client in some complicated case of corporate law; Jacob in South America or Spain, buying horses for his own ranch or for *El Sueño*, the family spread; Travis meeting with investors anywhere from Dallas to Singapore.

And there'd been times one or more of the Wildes had been ass-deep in some bug-infested foreign hellhole, trying to stay alive in whatever war needed the best combat helicopter pilot, secret agency spook, or jet jockey the U.S. of A. could provide.

There'd even been times a woman got in the way.

Travis lifted a bottle of beer to his lips.

That didn't happen often.

Women were wonderful and mysterious creatures, but brothers were, well, they were brothers. You shared the same blood, the same memories.

That made for something special.

The bottom line was that barring the end of the world and the appearance of the Four Horsemen of the Apocalypse, if it was Friday night, if the Wildes were within reasonable distance of each other, they'd find a bar where the brews were cold, the steaks rare, the music an upbeat blend of Willie Nelson and Bruce Springsteen, and they'd settle in for a couple of hours of relaxation.

This place didn't quite meet that description.

It wasn't where the Wildes had planned on going tonight but then, as it had turned out, Travis was the only Wilde who'd been up for getting together at all.

The original plan had been to meet at a bar they knew and liked, maybe half a dozen blocks from his office, a quiet place with deep booths, good music on the speakers, half a dozen varieties of locally-brewed beer on tap and by the bottle, and steaks the size of Texas sizzling on an open grill.

That plan had changed, and Travis had ended up in here by accident.

Once he knew he would be on his own, he'd driven around for a while, finally got thirsty and hungry, stopped at the first place he saw.

This one.

No deep booths. No Willy or Bruce. No locally-brewed beer. No grill and no steaks.

Instead, there were half a dozen beat-up looking tables and chairs. The kind of music that made your brain go numb, blasting from the speakers. A couple of brands of beer. Burgers oozing grease, served up from a kitchen in the back.

The best thing about the place was the bar itself, a long

stretch of zinc that either spoke of earlier, better days or of dreams that had never quite materialized.

Travis had pretty much known what he'd find as soon as he pulled into the parking lot, saw the dented pickups with their rusted fenders, the half a dozen Harleys parked together like a pack of coyotes.

He'd also known what he wouldn't find.

Friendly faces. Babes that looked as if they'd just stepped out of the latest Neiman Marcus catalogue. A dartboard on one wall, photos of local sports guys on another. St. Ambrose beer and rare steaks.

Not a great place for a stranger who was alone but if a man knew how to keep to himself, which years spent on not-always-friendly foreign soil had definitely taught him to do, he could at least grab something to eat before heading home.

He'd gotten some looks when he walked through the door. That figured. He was an unknown in a place where people almost certainly knew each other or at least recognized each other.

Physically, at least, he blended in.

He was tall. Six foot three in his bare feet, lean and muscled, the result of years riding and breaking horses growing up on *El Sueño,* the family's half-million acre ranch a couple of hours from Dallas. High school and college football had honed him to a tough edge, and Air Force training had done the rest.

At thirty-four, he worked out every morning in the gym in his Turtle Creek condo and he still rode most weekends, played pickup games of touch football with his brothers…

Correction, he thought glumly.

He used to play touch football with Caleb and Jacob, but they didn't have much time for that anymore.

Which was one of the reasons he was in this bar tonight. His brothers didn't have much time for anything anymore and, dammit, no, he wasn't feeling sorry for himself—he was a grown man, after all.

What he was, was mourning the loss of a way of life.

Travis tilted the bottle of Bud to his lips, took a long swallow and stared at his reflection in the fly-specked mirror behind the bar.

Bachelorhood. Freedom. No responsibility to or for anyone but yourself.

Yes, his brothers were giving life on the other side of that line a try and God knew, he wished them all the best but, though he'd never say it to them, he had a bad feeling how that would end up.

Love was an ephemeral emotion. Here today, gone tomorrow. Lip service, at best.

How his brothers had missed that life-lesson was beyond him.

He, at least, had not.

Which brought him straight back to what had been the old Friday night routine of steaks, beer…

And the one kind of bond you could count on.

The bond between brothers.

He'd experienced it growing up with Jake and Caleb, at college when he played football, in the Air Force, first in weeks of grueling training, then in that small, elite circle of men who flew fighter jets.

Male bonding, was the trendy media term for it, but you didn't need fancy words to describe the link of trust you could forge with a brother, whether by blood or by fate.

That was what those Friday nights had been about.

Sitting around, talking about nothing in particular—the safety the Cowboys had just signed. The wobbly fate of the Texas Rangers. Poker, a game they all liked and at which Travis was an expert. Which was more of an icon, Jake's vintage Thunderbird or Travis's '74 Stingray 'Vette, and was there any reasonable explanation for Caleb driving that disgustingly new Lamborghini?

And, naturally, they'd talked about women.

Except, the Wildes didn't talk about women anymore.

Travis sighed, raised the bottle again and drank.

Caleb and Jake. His brothers.

Married.

It still seemed impossible but it was true. So was what went with it.

He'd spoken with each of his brothers as recently as yesterday, reminded them—and when, in the past, had they needed reminding?—that Friday was coming up and they'd be meeting at seven at that bar near his office.

"Absolutely," Caleb had said.

"See you then," Jake had told him.

And here he was. The Lone Ranger.

The worst of it was, he wasn't really surprised.

No reflection on his sisters-in-law.

Travis was crazy about both Addison and Sage, loved them as much as he loved his own three sisters, but why deny it?

Marriage—commitment—changed everything.

"I can't make it tonight, Trav," Caleb had said when he'd phoned in midafternoon. We have Lamaze."

"Who?"

"It's not a who, it's a what. Lamaze. You know. Childbirth class. It's usually on Thursday but the instructor had to cancel so it's tonight, instead."

Childbirth class. His brother, the tough corporate legal eagle? The one-time spook? Childbirth class?

"Travis?" Caleb had said. "You there?"

"I'm here," he'd said briskly. "Lamaze. Right. Well, have fun."

"Lamaze isn't about fun, dude."

"I bet."

"You'll find out someday."

"Bite your tongue."

Caleb had laughed. "Remember that housekeeper we had right after Mom died? The one who used to say, *First comes love, then comes marriage...*"

Thinking back to the conversation, Travis shuddered.

Why would any of that ever apply to him?

Even if—big "if"—even if marriage worked, it changed a man.

Besides, love was just a nice word for sex, and why be modest?

He already had all the sex a man could handle, without any of the accompanying complications.

No "*I love you and I'll wait for you,*" which turned out to mean "*I'll wait a couple of months before I get into bed with somebody else.*"

Been there, done that, his first overseas tour.

Truth was, once he'd moved past the anger, it hadn't meant much. He'd been young; love had been an illusion.

And he should have known better, anyway, growing up in a home where your mother got sick and died and your father was too busy saving the world to come home and be with her or his sons...

And, dammit, what was with his mood tonight?

Travis looked up, caught the bartender's eye and signaled for another beer.

The guy nodded. "Comin' up."

Jake's phone call had followed on the heels of Caleb's.

"Hey," he'd said.

"Hey," Travis had replied, which didn't so much mark him as a master of brilliant dialogue as it suggested he knew what was coming.

"So," Jake had said, clearing his throat, "about getting together tonight—"

"You can't make it."

"Yes. I mean, no. I can't."

"Because?"

"Well, it turns out Addison made an appointment for us to meet with—with this guy."

"What guy?"

"Just a guy. About the work we've been doing, you know, remodeling the house."

"I thought that was your department. The extension, the extra bathrooms, the new kitchen—"

"It is. This guy does—he does other stuff."

"Such as?"

"Jeez, don't you ever give up? Such as recommending things."

"Things?"

"Wallpaper," Jake had all but snarled. "Okay? The guy's bringing over ten million wallpaper samples and Adoré told me about it days ago but I forgot and it's too late to—"

"Yeah. Okay. No problem," Travis had said because what right did he have to embarrass his war-hero brother more than he'd already embarrassed himself? The proof was right there, in Jake using his supposedly-unknown-to-the-rest-of-humanity pet name for his wife.

"Next week," Jake had said. "Right?"

Right, Travis thought, oh, yeah, right.

By next week, Caleb would be enrolled in Baby Burping 101 and Jake would be staring at fabric swatches, or whatever you called squares of cotton or velvet.

Domesticity was right up there with Lamaze.

Nothing he wanted to try.

Not ever.

He liked his life just the way it was, thank you very much. There was a big world out there, and he'd seen most of it—but not all. He still had places to go, things to do…

Things that might get the taste of war and death out of his mouth.

People talked about cleansing your palette between wine

tastings but nobody talked about cleansing your soul after piloting a jet into combat missions...

And, damn, what was he doing?

A flea-bitten bar in the wrong part of town absolutely was not the place for foolish indulgence in cheap philosophy.

Travis finished his beer.

Without being asked, the bartender opened a bottle, put it in front of him.

"Thanks."

"Haven't seen you in here before."

Travis shrugged. "First time for everything."

"You want somethin' to eat before the kitchen closes?"

"Sure. A steak, medium-rare."

"Your money, but the burgers are better."

"Fine. A burger. Medium-rare."

"Fries okay?"

"Fries are fine."

"Comin' right up."

Travis tilted the bottle to his lips.

A couple of weeks ago, his brothers had asked him what was doing with him. Was he feeling a little off lately?

"You're the ones who're off," he'd said with a quick smile. "Married. Living by the rules."

"Sometimes, rules are what a man needs," Jake had said.

"Yeah," Caleb had added. "You know, it might be time to reassess your life."

Reassess his life?

He liked his life just fine, thank you very much.

He needed precisely what he had. Life in the fast lane. Work hard. Play hard.

Nothing wrong with that.

It was how he'd always been.

His brothers, too, though war had changed them. Jake had, still was, battling through PTSD. Caleb carried a wariness inside him that would probably never go away.

Not him.

Sure, there were times he woke up, heart pounding, remembering stuff a man didn't want to remember, but a day at his office, taking a chance on a new stock offering and clearing millions as a result, a night in bed with a new, spectacular woman who was as uninterested in settling down as he was, and he was fine again.

Maybe that was the problem.

There hadn't been a woman lately.

And, now that he thought about it, what was with that? He wasn't into celibacy any more than he was into domesticity and yet, it had been days, hell, weeks since he'd been with a woman…

"Burger, medium-rare, with fries," the bartender said, sliding a huge plate across the bar.

Travis looked at the burger. It was the size of a Frisbee and burned to a crisp.

Good thing he wasn't really hungry, he thought, and he picked up a fry and took a bite.

The place was crowding up. Almost all the stools were taken at the bar; the same for the tables. The clientele, if you could call it that, was mostly male. Big. Tough-looking. Lots of facial hair, lots of tattoos.

Some of them looked him over.

Travis didn't hesitate to look back.

He'd been in enough places like this one, not just in Texas but in some nasty spots in eastern Europe and Asia, to know that you never flinched from eye contact.

It worked, especially because he didn't look like a weekend cowboy out for a night among the natives.

Aside from his height and build, which had come to him courtesy of Viking, Roman, Comanche and Kiowa ancestors, it helped that he'd given up his day-at-the-office custom-made Brioni suit for a well-worn gray T-shirt, equally well-worn jeans and a pair of Roper boots he'd had for years but then, why would any guy wear a suit and everything that went with it when he could be comfortable in jeans?

The clothes, the boots, his physical build, even his coloring—ink-black hair, courtesy of his Indian forebears, deep green eyes, thanks to his pillage-rape-and-romp European ancestors—all combined to make him look like, well, like what he was, a guy who wouldn't look for trouble but damned well wouldn't walk away from it if it came his way.

"A gorgeous, sexy, bad boy," one mistress had called him.

It had embarrassed the hell out of him—at least, that was what he'd claimed—but, hey, could a man fight his DNA?

The blood of generations of warriors pulsed in his veins, as it did in the veins of his brothers. Their father, the general, had raised them on tales of valor and courage and, in situations where it was necessary, the usefulness of an attitude that said don't-screw-with-me if you're smart.

It was a message men understood and generally respected, though there was almost always some jerk who thought it didn't apply to him.

That was fine.

It was equally fine that women understood it, too, and reacted to it in ways that meant he rarely spent a night alone, except by choice…

"Hi, honey."

Last time he'd checked, the barstool to his left had been empty. Not anymore. A blonde was perched on it, smiling as if she'd just found an unexpected gift under a Christmas tree.

Uh-oh.

She was surely a gift, too. For someone.

But that someone wasn't him.

To put it kindly, she wasn't his type.

Big hair that looked as if it had been shellacked into submission. Makeup she probably had to remove with a trowel. Tight cotton T-shirt, her boobs resting on a muffin-top of flesh forced up by too-tight jeans.

All that was bad enough.

What made it worse was that he knew the unspoken etiquette in a place like this.

A lady made a move on you, you were supposed to be flattered. Otherwise, you risked offending her—

Her, and the neighborhood *aficionados* who'd suddenly shifted their attention his way.

"Hello," he said with forced politeness, and then gave all his attention to his plate.

"You're new here."

Travis took a bite of hamburger, chewed as if chewing were the most important thing in his life.

"I'm Bev."

He nodded. Kept chewing.

She leaned in close, wedged one of her 40 Double D's against his arm.

"You got a name, cowboy?"

Now what? This was not a good situation. Whatever he did, short of taking Bev's clear invitation to heart, would almost surely lead to trouble.

She'd be insulted, her pals would think they had to ride to the rescue…

Maybe honesty, polite and up-front, was the best policy.

Travis took a paper napkin from its metal holder, blotted his lips and turned toward her.

"Listen, Bev," he said, not unkindly, "I'm not interested, okay?" Her face reddened and he thought, *hell, I'm not doing this right.* "I mean, you're a—a good-looking woman but I'm—I'm meeting somebody."

"Really?" Bev said coldly. "You want me to believe you're waitin' for your date?"

"Exactly. She'll be here any—"

"You're waitin' for your date, and you're eatin' without her?"

The guy on the other side of Bev was leaning toward them.

He was the size of a small mountain and from the look in his tiny eyes, he was hot and ready for a Friday night fight.

Slowly, carefully, Travis put down the burger and the napkin.

The Mountain outweighed him by fifty pounds, easy, and the hand wrapped around the bottle he was holding was the size of a ham.

No problem. Travis had taken on bigger men and come through just fine. If anything, it added to the kick.

Yes, but the Mountain has friends here. Many. And you, dude, are all by your lonesome.

The Voice of Reason.

Despite what his brothers sometimes said about him, Travis had been known not just to hear that voice but to listen to it.

But Bev was going on and on about no-good, scumbag liars and her diatribe had drawn the attention of several of the Mountain's pals. Every last one of them looked happy to come to her aid by performing an act of chivalry that would surely involve beating the outsider—him—into a bloody mass of barely-breathing flesh.

Not good, said the Voice of Reason.

The bloody part was okay. He'd been there before.

But there was a problem.

He had a meeting in Frankfurt Monday morning, a huge deal he'd been working on for months, and he had the not-very-surprising feeling that the board of directors at the ultraconservative, three-hundred-year-old firm of Bernhardt, Bernhardt and Stutz would not look kindly on a financial expert who showed up with a couple of black eyes, a dinged jaw and, for all he knew, one or two missing teeth.

It would not impress them at all if he explained that he'd done his fair share of damage. More than his fair share, because he surely would manage that.

Dammit, where were a man's brothers when he needed them?

"The lady's talkin' to you." The Mountain was leaning past Bev. God, his breath stank. "What's the matter? You got a hearin' problem or something, pretty boy?"

Conversation died out. People smiled.

Travis felt the first, heady pump of adrenaline.

"My name," he said carefully, "is not 'pretty boy.'"

"His name is not pretty boy," The Mountain mimicked.

Bev, sporting a delighted smile, slid from her stool. Maybe he'd misjudged her purpose. Maybe setting up a fight had been her real job.

Either way, Travis saw his choices narrowing down, and rapidly.

Bev's defender got to his feet.

"You're making a mistake," Travis said quietly.

The Mountain snorted.

Travis nodded, took a last swig of beer, said a mental "goodbye" to Monday's meeting and stood up.

"Outside," he said, "in the parking lot? Or right here?"

"Here," a voice growled.

Three men had joined the Mountain. Travis smiled. The next five minutes might be the end of him.

Yeah, but they'd also be fun, especially considering his weird state of mind tonight.

"Fine," he said. "Sounds good to me."

Those words, the commitment to the inevitable, finalized things, sent his adrenaline not just pumping but racing. He hadn't been in a down-and-dirty bar brawl in a very long time. Not since Manila, or maybe Kandahar.

Yes, Kandahar, his last mission, death all around him...

Suddenly, pounding the Mountain into pulp seemed a fine idea, never mind that deal in Frankfurt.

Besides, nothing short of a miracle could save him now...

The door to the street swung open.

For some reason Travis would never later be able to explain, the enraptured audience watching him and the Mountain turned toward it.

A blast of hot Texas air swept in.

So did a tall, beautiful, sexy-looking, straight-out-of-the-Neiman-Marcus-catalogue blonde.

Silence. Complete silence.

Everybody looked at Neiman Marcus.

Neiman Marcus looked at them.

And blanched.

"Well, lookee there," somebody said.

Lookee, indeed, Travis thought.

Sanity returned.

There she was. His salvation.

"Finally," he said, his tone bright and cheerful. "My date."

Before anyone could say a word, he started toward the blonde and the door with the confidence of a man holding all four aces in a game of high stakes poker.

She tilted her head back as he got closer. She was tall, especially in sexy, nosebleed-high stilettos, but she still had to do that to look up at him.

He liked it.

It was a nice touch.

"Your what?" she said, or would have said, but he couldn't afford to let things go that far.

"Baby," he purred, "what took you so long?"

Her eyes widened. "Excuse me?"

Travis grinned.

"Only if you ask real nice," he said, and before she could react, he drew her into his arms, brought her tightly against him and covered her mouth with his.

CHAPTER TWO

AN HOUR BEFORE she walked into Travis Wilde's life, Jennie Cooper had been sitting in her ancient Civic, having a stern talk with herself.

By then, it had been close to nine o'clock, the evening wasn't getting any younger, and she still hadn't put her plan into action.

Ridiculous, of course.

She was a woman with a mission.

She was looking for a bar.

Really, how difficult could it be to find a bar in a city like Dallas?

Very.

Well, "very" if you were searching for just the right kind of bar.

Dallas was a big, sprawling town, and she'd driven through so many parts of it that she'd lost count.

She'd started with Richardson and though there were loads of bars in that area, it would have been foolish, better still, foolhardy to choose one of them.

It was too near the university campus.

So she'd headed for the Arts District, mostly because she knew it, if visiting a couple of galleries on a rainy Sunday qualified as "knowing" a place—after eight months, she was still learning about her new city—but as soon as she got there, she'd realized it, too, was a bad choice.

The Arts District was trendy, which meant she'd feel out of place. A laugh, really, considering that she was going to feel out of place no matter where she went tonight, but it was also a neighborhood that surely would be popular with university faculty.

Running into someone who knew her would be disaster.

That was when Jennie had pulled to the curb, put her wheezing Civic in neutral and told herself to think fast, before her plan fell apart.

What other parts of Dallas were there?

Turtle Creek.

She knew it only by reputation, and that it was home to lots of young, successful, rich professionals.

Well, she'd thought with what might have been a choked laugh, she was young, anyway.

Rich? Not on a teaching assistant's stipend. Successful? Not in Turtle Creek terms, where the word surely referred to attorneys and doctors, financial gurus and industrialists.

What kind of small talk could she make with a man who was all those things, assuming such a man would look twice at her?

Assuming there'd be any small talk because, really, that wasn't what tonight was all about.

The realization sent a bolt of terror zinging along her nerve endings.

Jennie fought against it.

She wasn't scared.

Certainly not.

She was—she was anxious, and who wouldn't be? She'd spent weeks and weeks, planning this—this event.

She wasn't going to add to that anxiety by going to a bar in a place like Turtle Creek on a Friday night when—when singles mingled.

When singles hook up, Genevieve baby, her always-until-now-oh-so-logical alter ego had suddenly whispered.

"They mingle," Jennie had muttered. "And my name is not—"

Except, it was. For tonight. She'd decided that the same time she'd hatched this plan.

Good. You remembered. You're Genevieve. And you're trying to pretty things up. Tonight is not about mingling, it is about—

Jennie had stopped listening.

Still, there was truth to it.

Nobody could pretty this up.

Her plan was basic.

Find a bar. Go inside. Order a drink. Find a man she liked, flirt with him…

Forget the metaphors.

What she wanted was to find a man she liked enough to take home to bed.

Her teeth chattered.

"Stop it," she said sharply.

She was a grown woman. Twenty-four years old just last Sunday. That she had never slept with a man was disgraceful. It was worse than that.

It was unbelievable.

And the old Stones song lied.

Time wasn't on her side, which was why she was going to remedy that failing tonight.

"Happy birthday to me," she said, under her breath, and her teeth did the castanet thing again, which was ridiculous.

She had thought about this for a long time, examined the concept from every possible angle.

This was right. It was logical. It was appropriate.

It was how things had to be done.

No romance. This wasn't about romance.

No attachment. That part wasn't even worth analyzing.

She didn't have time for attachment, or emotion, or anything but the experience.

That was what this was all about.

It was research. It was learning something you'd only read about.

It was no different from what she'd done in the past, driving from New Hampshire to New York before she wrote her senior paper so that she could experience what had once been the narrow streets where Stanton Coit had established a settlement house for immigrants long before there were such things as social workers, or the trip she'd planned to see the Jane Addams Hull-House Museum in Chicago…

Her throat constricted.

Never mind all that.

Her days of academic research would soon be meaningless.

What she needed now was reality research, and if there wasn't such a branch of study, there should be.

And she was wasting precious time.

Jennie checked both rearview mirrors, put on her signal light and pulled away from the curb.

She headed south.

After a while, the streets began to change.

They grew narrower. Darker. The houses were smaller, crammed together as if huddled against a starless Texas night.

The one good thing was that there were lots of bars.

Lots and lots of bars.

She drove past them all.

Of course, she did.

None passed muster.

One didn't have enough vehicles parked outside.

One had too many.

One had the wrong kind.

Jennie's alter-ego gave an impolite snort. Jennie couldn't blame her. That made three out of three.

What was she, Goldilocks?

Okay. The very next bar would be The One. In caps. Definitely, The One.

She'd park, check her hair, her makeup—she'd never used this much makeup before and, ten to one, it was smeared...

BAR.

Her heart thumped.

There it was. Straight ahead. A bar called, appropriately enough, **BAR**. Well, no. That wasn't its name—she was pretty sure of that—it was simply a description, like a sign saying "liquor" outside a liquor store, or one that said "motel" outside a motel, or...

For God's sake, Genevieve, it's a bar!

She slowed the car, turned on her signal light, checked the mirrors, waited patiently for an approaching vehicle a block away to pass before she pulled into the parking lot.

It was crowded.

The last available empty space was between a shiny black behemoth of a truck and a battered red van.

She pulled between them, opened her door, checked the faded white lines, saw that she hadn't managed to center her car, shut the door, backed up carefully, shifted, pulled forward, checked again, backed up, checked one last time, saw she'd finally parked properly and shut off the engine.

Tick, tick, tick it said, and finally went silent.

Too silent.

She could hear her heart thudding.

Stop it!

Quickly, she opened her consignment-shop Dior purse, rummaged inside it, found her compact and flipped it open.

She'd spent twenty minutes this afternoon at Neiman Marcus, nervously wandering around among the endless cosmetic counters before she'd finally chosen one mostly because the clerk behind it looked a shade less unapproachable than the others.

"How may I help you, miss?" she'd said. "Foundation? Blusher? Eyebrows? Eyes? Lips? Hair? Skin?"

Translation: *Sweetie, you need work!*

But her smile had been pleasant and Jennie had taken a deep breath and said, "Do you do makeovers?"

Almost an hour later, the clerk—she was, she'd said, a cosmetician—put a big mirror in her hands and said, "Take a look."

Jennie had looked.

Nobody she knew looked back.

Who was this person with the long, loose blond waves framing her face? When had her pale lashes become curly and dark? And that pouting pink mouth, those cheekbones...

Cheekbones?

"Wow," she'd said softly.

The cosmetician had grinned.

"Wow, indeed. Your guy is gonna melt when he sees you tonight."

"No. I mean, that's just the point. I don't have—"

"So," the cosmetician had chirped, "what do we want to purchase?"

"Purchase?" Jennie had said, staring at the lineup of vials, bottles and tubes, the sprays, salves and brushes, even an instruction sheet about how to replicate the magic transformation. Her gaze had flown to the woman. "I can't possibly..." She'd swallowed hard, pointed to a tube of thirty-dollar mascara and said, "I'll take that."

Nobody was happy. Not the cosmetics wizard. Not Jennie, whose last mascara purchase had cost her six bucks at the supermarket.

Had all that time and money been worth it?

It was time to find out.

Even in the badly lit parking lot, her mirror assured her that she looked different.

It also assured her that she was wearing a mask.

Well, a disguise. Which was good.

It made her feel as if she was what she'd been trained to be, a researcher. An observer. An academic who would spend the next hours in a different kind of academia than she was accustomed to.

Jennie snapped the compact shut and put it back in her purse.

Which was why she was parked outside this place with the blinking neon sign.

Upscale? No. The lot was full of pickup trucks. She knew by now that pickup trucks were Texas the same way four-wheel drives were New England, but most of these were old. There were motorcycles, too.

Weren't motorcycles supposed to be sexy?

And there were lots of lighted beer signs in the window.

Downscale? Well, as compared to what? True, something about the place didn't seem appealing.

It's a bar, the dry voice inside her muttered. *What are you, a scout for* Better Homes and Gardens?

Still, was this a good choice? She'd worked up logical criteria.

A: Choose a place that drew singles. She knew what happened in singles bars. Well, she'd heard what happened, anyway—that they were where people went for uninhibited fun, drinking, dancing…and other things.

B: Do what she was going to do before summer changed to autumn.

C: Actually, it had not occurred to her there might be a part C. But there was.

Do Not Prevaricate.

And she was prevaricating.

She put away her compact. Opened the door. Stepped from the car. Shut the door. Locked it. Opened her purse. Put her keys inside. Closed the purse. Hung the thin strap over the shoulder of her equally thin-strapped emerald-green silk dress, bought from the same consignment shop as the purse, the Neiman Marcus tag still inside.

Assuming you could call something that stopped at midthigh a dress.

She knew it was.

Girls on campus wore dresses this length.

You're not a girl on campus, Jennie. And even when you were, back in New Hampshire, you never wore anything that looked like this.

And maybe if she had, she wouldn't be doing this tonight. She wouldn't have to be looking for answers to questions that needed answers, questions she was running out of time to ask…

"Stop," she whispered.

It was time to get moving.

She took a breath, then started walking toward the entrance to the bar, stumbling a little in the sky-high heels she'd also bought at the consignment shop.

She was properly turned out, from head to toe, to lure the kind of man she wanted into her bed. Somebody tall. Broad-shouldered. A long, lean, buff body. Dark hair, dark eyes, a gorgeous face because if you were going to lose your virginity to a stranger, if this was going to be your One and Only sexual experience, Jennie thought as she put her hand on the door to the bar and pushed it open, if this was going to be It, you wanted the man to be…

Was that music?

It was loud. Very loud. What was it? She had no idea. Telling Tchaikovsky from Mozart was one thing. Telling rock from rock was another.

She caught her bottom lip between her teeth.

Maybe she was making a mistake.

Yes, the place was far from the university. She wouldn't see anyone she knew, but what about the rest? Was it a singles bar? Or was it—what did people call them? A tavern? A neighborhood place where people came to drink?

Such a dark street. Such an unprepossessing building. That neon sign, even the asphalt because now that she'd seen it, close-up, she could see that it was cracked…

That's enough!

She'd talked herself out of a dozen other possibilities. She was not talking herself out of this one.

Chin up, back straight—okay, one last hand smoothing her hair, one last tug at her dress and she really should have chosen one that covered her thighs…

Jennie reached for the door, yanked it open…

And stepped into a sensory explosion.

The music pulsed off the walls, vibrated through the floor.

The smell was awful. Yeasty, kind of like rising bread dough but not as pleasant, and under it, the smell of things frying in grease.

And the noise! People shouting over the music. What sounded like hundreds of them. Not really; there weren't hundreds of people at the long bar, at the handful of tables, but there were lots of them…And they were mostly male.

Some were wearing leather.

Maybe she'd made a mistake. Wandered into a gay…

No. These guys weren't gay. They were—they were unattractive. Lots of facial hair. Lots of tattoos. Lots of big bellies overhanging stained jeans.

There were a few women, but that didn't help. The women were—big. Big hair. Big boobs. Big everything.

People were looking at her.

Indeed they are, Genevieve. That's what people do, when a woman all dressed up walks into a place like this.

Oh, God. Even her alter-ego thought she'd made a mistake!

Her heart leaped into her throat. She wanted to turn around and go right out the door.

But it was too late.

A man was walking toward her.

Not walking. Sauntering, was more accurate, his long stride slow and easy, more than a match for his lazy smile.

Her breath caught.

His eyes were dark. His hair was the color of rich, dark coffee. It was thick, and longer than a man's hair should be, longer, anyway, than the way men in her world wore it, and she had the swift, almost overwhelming desire to bury her hands in it.

Plus, he was tall.

Tall and long and lean and muscled.

You could almost sense the hard delineation of muscle in his wide shoulders and arms and chest, and—and she was almost certain he had a—what did you call it? A six-pack, that was it. A six-pack right there, in his middle.

A middle that led down to—down to his lower middle.

To more muscle, a different kind of muscle, hidden behind faded denim…

Her cheeks burned.

Her gaze flew up again, over, what, all six foot two, six foot three of him. Flew up over worn boots, jeans that fit his long legs and narrow hips like a second skin, a T-shirt that clung to his torso.

Their eyes met.

Tall as she was, especially in the stilettos, she had to look up for that to happen.

He smiled.

Her mouth went dry. He was, in a word, gorgeous.

"Baby," he said in a husky voice. "What took you so long?"

Huh?

Nobody knew she'd been coming here tonight. She hadn't even known it herself, until she'd pulled into the parking lot.

"Excuse me?"

His smile became a grin. Could grins be sexy and hot? Oh yes. Yes, they could.

"Only if you ask real nice," he said, and then, without any warning, she was in his arms and his mouth was on hers.

CHAPTER THREE

TRAVIS LIKED WOMEN.

In bed, of course. Sex was one of life's great pleasures.
But he liked them in other ways, too.

Their scent. Their softness. Those Mona Lisa smiles that
could keep a man guessing for hours, even days.

And all the things that were part of sex…

He could never have enough of those.

He knew, from years of locker-room talk, that some men
saw kissing as nothing but a distraction from the main event.

Not him.

Kissing was something that deserved plenty of time. He
loved exploring a woman's taste, the silken texture of her lips,
the feel of them as they parted to the demand of his.

Women liked it, too.

Enough of them had mingled their sighs with his, melted
in his arms, parted their lips to the silken thrust of his tongue
to convince him—why not be honest?—that he was a man
skilled at the act.

Tonight, none of that mattered.

The blonde was attractive—the ruse wouldn't work if she
weren't—but there was nothing personal involved.

Kissing her was a means to an end, a way to get him out
of a confrontation in a Dallas dive to a boardroom in Frank-

furt without looking as if he'd gone ten rounds in a bar exactly like this one.

The key to success? He'd known he'd have to move fast, take her by surprise, kiss her hard enough to silence any protest.

With luck, she'd go along with the game.

Far more exotic things happened in bars everywhere than a man stealing a kiss.

Besides, a woman who looked like this, who walked into a place like this, wasn't naive.

For all he knew, she was out slumming.

A kiss from a stranger might be just the turn-on she wanted.

And if she protested, he'd play to his audience, pretend it was all about her being ticked off at him for some imagined lover's slight.

Either way, he wasn't going to give her, or them, a lot of time to think about it.

He'd kiss her, then hustle her outside where he could explain it had all been a game and either thank her for her cooperation or apologize for what he'd done...or maybe, just maybe, she'd laugh and what the hell, the night was still young.

Bottom line?

Kissing her was all he had to work with, so he flashed his best smile, the one that never failed to thaw a woman's defenses, reached out, put his arms around her, gathered her in...

Her eyes widened. She slapped both hands against his chest.

"What do you think you're doing?"

Travis showed her.

He captured her lips with his.

For nothing longer than a second, he thought he was home

free. Sure, she stiffened against him, said *"Mmmff"* or something close to it, but he could work with that.

The problem?

She went crazy in his arms.

It would have done his ego good to think she'd gone crazy with pleasure.

But she hadn't.

She went crazy the way he'd once seen his sister Em do when she'd bent down to pick up what she'd thought was a compact and found herself, instead, with a handful of tarantula.

The blonde in his arms jerked against him. Pounded his shoulders with her fists. Said that *"Mmmff"* thing again and again and again...

Somebody laughed.

Somebody said, "What the hell's he doin'?"

Somebody else said, "Damned if ah know."

What Travis knew was that this was not good.

"I'm not trying to hurt you," he snarled, his mouth a breath from Blondie's.

"Mmmff!"

She struggled harder. Lifted her foot. Put one of those stiletto heels into his instep and it was a damn good thing he was wearing boots.

He put his lips to her ear.

"Lady. Listen to what I'm saying. I'm not—"

Big mistake.

"Help," she yelled, or would have yelled—he could see her lips forming the sound of that "h"—so, really, what choice did he have?

He kissed her again.

This time, her knee came up.

He felt it coming, twisted to avoid it, then hung on to her for dear life.

The crowd hooted.

Jeez, was he going to be the night's entertainment?

"Lady sure do seem happy to see you, cowboy," the Mountain shouted.

Everybody roared with laughter.

Okay.

This called for a different approach.

Travis thrust one hand into Blondie's hair, clamped the other at the base of her spine, tilted her backward over his arm just enough to keep her off balance and brushed his lips over hers.

Once. Twice. Three times, each time ignoring that angry *Mmmff.*

"Don't fight me," he whispered between kisses. "Just make this look real and I swear, I'll let you go."

No *mmmff* that time. Nothing but a little sighing sound...

And the softest, most delicate whisper of her breath.

"Good girl," Travis murmured, and he changed the angle of his mouth on hers...

God, she tasted sweet.

Slowly he drew her erect. Put both hands into her hair. Kissed her a little harder.

She tasted like sunshine on a soft June morning, smelled like wildflowers after a summer rain.

His arms went around her; he gathered her against the hardness of his body, felt the softness of her breasts and belly against him.

The crowd cheered.

Travis barely heard them.

He was lost in what was happening, the feel of the woman in his arms, the race of her heart against his.

An urgency he'd never felt before raced through him.

He was on fire.

So was she.

She was trembling. Whimpering. She was—

Sweet Lord.

The truth hit. Hard. She wasn't on fire for him, she was terrified.

She hadn't acquiesced to his kisses, she'd stopped fighting them.

What kind of SOB did this to a woman? Scared the life out of her, and all to save his own sorry ass?

All at once, the trip to Frankfurt lost its meaning. He was a financial wizard but what he really was, was a gambler. He'd lost money before; he'd lose it again.

Millions were on the line.

So what?

When had winning become so important he'd use someone—not just "someone" but a woman—to make sure the dice rolled the way he wanted?

He lifted his head. Looked down into the face of the woman in his arms.

His gut twisted.

Her skin was pale, the color all but completely drained away. Her breathing was swift; he could see the rapid pulse fluttering in her throat. Her eyes—her eyes, he knew, would haunt him forever. They were beautiful eyes, but now they had turned dark with fear.

"Oh, honey," he said softly.

She shook her head. "Don't," she said in a tiny whisper. "Please. Don't—"

He kissed her again, but lightly, tenderly, his lips barely moving against hers.

"I'm sorry," he said. "I never meant to frighten you."

There was a whisper of sound behind him. He was giving the game away. Screw it. Screw whatever would happen next. All he wanted was to get that look of fear off the blonde's lovely face.

"Lovely" didn't come close.

That cloud of silken hair. The dark blue eyes. The soft, rosy mouth.

She was still shaking.

No way was he going to let that continue.

"I'm not going to hurt you," he said. "I never intended to hurt you." Her face registered disbelief, and Travis shook his head. "It's the truth, honey. This was never about you. Not the way you think." He framed her face with his hands, raised it just a little so he was looking directly into her eyes. "I ran into a problem. With some people here."

"Damn right," the Mountain growled.

Travis heard him hawk up a glob of spit, heard it hit the floor.

The blonde looked past his shoulder, her eyes widening. She looked at Travis again. Two slender parallel lines appeared between her eyebrows.

"See, I told them I was waiting for my date—"

"Thass what he said," one of the Mountain's pals said. "But we knew he was lyin'—an' we know what to do with liars."

A loud rumble of assent greeted the proclamation.

The blonde's gaze swept past Travis again. Her eyes filled with comprehension.

"And then," Travis said, ignoring the interruption, "then, the door opened and you walked in. One look and I knew that you were right for me, that you were perfect, that you were—"

"The woman you'd been waiting for," the blonde said, very softly.

He smiled, a little sadly because there was no question how this was going down. The only thing he needed to do now was get her safely out of here because however she'd come to be at this bar tonight, she was definitely in the wrong place at the wrong time.

"Exactly right, honey. You were just the woman I'd have waited for, and—"

The blonde put her finger over his lips.

"Of course I was," she said, her voice louder now, loud enough to carry to the men behind Travis. "How foolish of you to think that I wasn't going to keep our date, just because I showed up a bit late."

This time, Travis was the one whose eyes widened.

"What?"

"I was angry, I admit. That quarrel we had last week? About—about me thinking you'd been with another woman?" She smiled. "I know I was wrong. You wouldn't cheat on me, not ever."

For mercy's sake, man, say something!

"Uh—uh, no. I mean, you're right. I wouldn't. Cheat on you. Ever."

She nodded.

"But I couldn't just admit that." Another smile, this one half-vixen, half-innocent. "It's against all the precepts of male-female genetically-transmitted courtship behavior."

The what?

"So I decided to keep you waiting tonight. Let you cool your heels a little, kind of wonder if I was going to show up." Another smile, this one so hot and sexy Travis felt his knees go weak. "And you did wonder, didn't you? About me and how I'd deal with our date this evening."

Travis tried to answer. Nothing happened. He cleared his throat and tried again.

"Yes. Right. I surely did. Wonder, I mean, about how you'd deal with our—"

"And you reacted to perfection! Every single DNA-coded response was in evidence. Machismo. Dominance. Aggression. Even an attempt at territorial marking."

Territorial marking. Wasn't that about male dogs peeing on trees?

"I am so pleased," she said, "that you've proved the tenets of my paper."

"Your paper."

"Oh, yes, exactly! The way you reacted on seeing me, the way you dealt with my less-than-warm greeting…"

There was a hum behind him. Whispers. Snorts. Laughter.

It was, without question, time to move on.

Travis nodded. "That's great. It's terrific. But I really think we should discuss the rest of it out—"

"Why, sugar," the blonde all but purred, "don't tell me you're upset by learning you've helped my research!"

Not just laughter, but a couple of deep guffaws greeted that pronouncement.

Definitely time, Travis thought, holding his smile as he took the blonde by the elbow and marched her to the door.

Halfway there, Jennie's alter-ego snickered.

Should have quit while you were ahead, Genevieve, it said.

Indeed, Jennie thought. She should have.

The stranger who'd kissed her was hurrying her toward the door.

Maybe she'd taken this a bit too far.

She had, if the look on the man's face was any indication.

His eyes were cool. Slate-cool, and a little scary. His mouth—she knew all about his mouth, the warmth of it, the possessive feel of it, the taste—his mouth was curved in what was surely a phony smile, and he was hustling her along at breakneck speed.

Still, he'd deserved that last little jibe.

Saving him from being torn apart by that bunch of—of stone-age savages was one thing, but she couldn't just let him get away with what he'd done.

He'd scared the life half out of her, grabbing her, kissing her, dragging her up against his body.

And, yes, she'd come out tonight for—for that knowledge of men, of kisses, of hard bodies but she'd wanted it done on her own terms, at her own pace, with her doing the choosing of the man who'd—who'd complete her research.

A man in a suit. A successful executive, someone who

could be trusted to be gentle with a woman. Not a—a rough-and-ready cowboy in boots and a T-shirt and faded jeans.

Stop complaining. You wanted gorgeous, and gorgeous is what he is.

Yes. But still—

"Y'all come back soon," a voice called.

A roar of laughter followed the words.

She felt the cowboy stiffen beside her. His fingers dug into her elbow hard enough to make her gasp.

"Hey," she said indignantly, "hey—"

He flung the door open, stepped outside, but he didn't let go of her. Instead he frog-marched her through the parking lot to the enormous black pickup parked next to her Civic.

"Mister. I am not—"

"Are you okay?"

Jennie blinked. There was concern in his voice, and it wasn't what she'd expected.

"No. Yes. I guess…"

"That was a close call. You were doin' fine, until the end." He grinned. "Had to zing me a little, right? Not that I blame you."

"You? Blame *me*?" Indignation colored her voice. "Listen, mister—"

"Truth is, we probably got out just in time."

So much for indignation, which didn't stand a chance against confusion.

"In time for what?" Jennie said. "What was going on back there?"

"It's kind of complicated." The cowboy smiled. This time, that smile was real. "Thanks for digging me out of a deep, dark hole."

"Well, well, you're welcome. I guess. I just don't understand what—"

"It's not worth going into. It was a mix-up, was all."

He smiled again. Jennie's heart leaped. Did he have any idea how devastatingly sexy that smile was?

She told herself to say something. Anything. Gawking at him wasn't terribly sophisticated. But then, what would he know about sophistication? The boots, the jeans, the hard muscles…

Everything about him was hard.

The muscled chest. The taut abdominals. The—the male part of him that she'd felt press against her belly just before he'd stopped kissing her…

That's the girl, her alter ego said.

Jennie swallowed dryly.

Her brain was going in half a dozen directions at once.

"You—you really had no right to—to just walk up to me and…and—"

"—and kiss you?"

She felt herself blush.

"Yes. Exactly. Even in the most highly sexualized primitive cultures, there's a certain decorum involved in expressing desire…"

His smile tilted.

"Is there," he said.

It wasn't a question—it was a statement. And the way he was looking at her…

She took a quick step back.

Or she would have taken a quick step back, but the shiny black truck was right behind her.

"The point is," she said, trying to focus on why she was angry at him, "you shouldn't have done what you did."

"Kissed you, without so much as a 'hello.'"

"Right. Precisely. The proper protocol, prior to intimacy—"

Jennie stopped in mid-sentence. She sounded like an idiot. Even her alter-ego had crept away in embarrassment.

"Never mind," she said quickly. "It's late. And I—"

"Travis," he said. "Travis Wilde."

She stared at him. "Pardon me?"

He smiled. Again. And her heart jumped again.

"My name." His voice had gone low and husky. "I'm introducing myself. That would have been the proper protocol, wouldn't it?"

"Well, yes, but—"

"And your name is…?"

"Oh."

She swallowed hard. Again. She was not good at this. At male-female banter. At any of it.

"I could call you Blondie." He reached out, caught a strand of her hair between his fingers, smoothed its silken length. "Or Neiman Marcus."

"What?" Jennie looked down at herself. "Is the dress tag show—"

"That's how you look," he said softly. "As if you just stepped out of their catalogue. Their Christmas catalogue, the one that always has the prettiest things in it."

Her knees were going to buckle.

His voice was like a caress.

His eyes were like hot coals.

He was—he was just what she'd been looking for, hoping for—

"But I'd rather call you by your real name, if you'll tell it to me."

"It's Jen…It's Genevieve," she whispered. "My name is Genevieve."

"Well, Genevieve, you did a foolish thing tonight."

God, she could feel herself blushing again!

"Listen here, Mr. Wills—"

"Wilde. Travis Wilde."

"Listen here, Mr. Wilde. I only let you kiss me after I realized you were going to get killed if I didn't!"

He chuckled.

Even his chuckle was sexy.

"I was talking about you going into that bar in the first place."

"Oh."

"Oh, for sure. You have any idea what kind of bunch you were dealing with back there?"

"I—I—" Jennie sighed. "No."

"I didn't think so. But it's lucky for me you walked in."

"It certainly is," she said, lifting her chin. "Or you'd be just another stain on that already-stained floor."

He grinned. "Yeah, but a happy stain."

"That's so typical! Men and their need to assert power through dominance—"

"Men and their need to save their tails, honey. Ordinarily I wouldn't have bothered, but I have something going down Monday, and the last thing I need is to show up lookin' like the winner of a bare-knuckles fight."

"You couldn't have won. There were too many of them."

"Of course I could have won," he said, so easily that she knew he meant it.

A little tremor went through her.

She'd come out tonight in search of a man. And she'd found one. But he was—he was more than she'd anticipated.

More than handsome.

More than sexy.

More than macho.

And more than everything you'd want in bed, her alter-ego purred.

Jennie tried to step back again.

"Well," she said brightly, "it's been—it's been interesting, Mr. Wilde. Now, if you don't mind—"

"About those protocols," he said, his voice low, his tone husky, "have we met them all?"

"The what?"

"The protocols. The ones needed before any kind of intimacy."

The woman named Genevieve blushed.

Again.

She did that, a lot.

Travis liked it.

Would her face and breasts turn that same shade of soft pink during sex? Would her eyes lock on his the way they were now, dark and wide but filled with passion instead confusion?

Crazy as it was, the fate of the world seemed to hinge on learning the answer.

"Because if we've met those protocols," he said, moving closer, flattening his palms against the cab of the truck so that his arms encased her, "I'd like to take the next step."

"What next—what next—"

He looked into her eyes. Looked at her lips. Gave her a second to figure out what was coming.

"No," she whispered.

"Yes," he said, and in what seemed like slow motion, he lowered his head to hers and took her mouth.

Her lips parted. His tongue slipped between them. Her heart banged into her throat. The taste of him, the feel of him inside her mouth...

Ohmygod, she thought, *oh—my—God!*

He groaned.

His arms went around her.

Hers rose and wound around his neck.

She pressed herself against him. And gasped.

He was hard as a rock.

She wanted to rub against him. Wanted to move her hips against his. Wanted to—to—

He lifted her off the ground, one arm around her waist, the other just below her backside. Her face was on a level with his; he kissed her slowly, caught her bottom lip between his teeth and sucked on her flesh, and—and—

A dazzling jolt of pure desire shot through her, the same as it had for one amazing moment in the bar, when her fear and indignation had given way to something very, very different. Something she'd refused to admit, even to herself.

"Wait," she whispered, but he didn't and she didn't want him to wait, didn't want anything to wait even though this wasn't going according to plan.

He set her down, slowly, on her feet.

Don't stop, she thought.

He didn't.

He put his hands on her.

On her hips, bringing her, hard, against his erection.

On her breasts, oh, on her breasts, his thumbs dancing with tantalizing slowness over her nipples.

"What," she whispered breathlessly, "what are you doing?"

His laugh was low and husky and so filled with sexual promise that she almost moaned.

"What does it feel like I'm doing?"

She swallowed dryly. "It feels like—like you're making love to me."

"Good." He kissed her throat. "Because that's exactly what I am doing, Genevieve. What I want to go on doing."

He kissed the place where her neck and shoulder joined.

It was magic.

Her eyes closed; the world went away.

And when he asked her to go home with him, she gave him the only logical answer because, after all, she was nothing if not logical.

She said, "Yes."

CHAPTER FOUR

THE 'VETTE WOULD have been faster but Travis was driving his pickup tonight and the GMC Denali, modified to his specifications, was as fast as anything on the road that was street-legal.

Besides, his condo was only half an hour away.

Still, that half an hour seemed like an eternity.

Travis was having a tough time keeping his hands off the woman seated beside him.

Why wouldn't he?

He was in the prime of life, a sexually active, heterosexual male, and their meeting had been just unusual enough to have an edge of excitement.

Still, there was something almost primal in his hunger for her—for Genevieve—and he knew it.

He'd come close to taking her against the truck, right there in the parking lot.

There was something to be said for spur-of-the-moment sex in unexpected places but sex outside a bar filled with a bunch of what might charitably be called yahoos wasn't high on the list.

Besides, he wanted more than quick relief.

He wanted…

Who knew what he wanted tonight?

Had he gone into that bar looking for trouble?

As a boy, football had been an outlet for the anger he'd sometimes felt at his father for spending more time with the young men who served under him than with his own sons, even after their mother's death.

In Afghanistan, once he'd figured out that he was fighting in a war governed by politics and not morality, he'd taken to long, punishing runs across the hot desert sand.

So, tonight, was he angry at his brothers for abandoning him? For the changes in his life…

Hell.

What kind of thoughts were those to have when a beautiful woman was with him, a woman whose feel and taste promised paradise?

Maybe he was wrong. Maybe what he needed was quick relief, that moment when you sank into a woman's softness and heat…

Dammit.

He kept thinking like this, things would be over before they got started.

Ahead, a traffic light went from green to amber. He stepped down even harder on the gas and shot through the intersection before the light changed again.

Only another couple of blocks to go.

Genevieve was quiet. In fact, she hadn't said a word since they'd gotten into the Denali.

He glanced at her. She was sitting up very straight in the leather bucket seat, eyes straight ahead, hands folded in her lap.

Hands that were trembling.

Was she having second thoughts?

"Hey," he said softly.

She looked at him, then away. He reached over, put his hand over hers. Her skin was icy.

Was she frightened? It didn't seem possible, not after the

way she'd responded to him in the parking lot, but he'd lived long enough to know that anything was possible.

He wrapped his hand around hers, held on until her fingers unknotted and he could bring her hand to rest under his on the gearshift.

"We're almost there."

She nodded. And caught her bottom lip between her teeth.

His body tightened at the sight.

"I live in Turtle Creek. Near Lee Park."

She didn't answer. Why would she? What was he, a Realtor taking a client to see a property? If only she'd say something...

And how come he was taking her to his bed?

He wasn't big on taking his lovers home with him. Not that this woman was going to be his lover but...

Why was he making this so complicated?

Travis cleared his throat.

"Did you—would you like to stop first? For a drink? For something to eat?"

She stared at him. Why wouldn't she? He knew, she knew, what was going to happen next and in the middle of all that, he was going to, what, stop at a diner?

Maybe.

He flashed a quick smile.

"It just hit me, we blew past the 'hello, how are you' formalities. So, if you'd like to stop at a restaurant—"

She moistened her lips with the tip of her tongue. His body tightened in response.

"No."

Her voice was low, but her answer was clear.

She wanted him as much as he wanted her.

It was a good thing his place was directly ahead.

He slowed the truck. Hit the button that opened the garage doors. Drove inside. Hit the button that closed the doors...

And thought, to hell with waiting, undid his seat belt, reached over and undid hers and drew her into his arms.

"Genevieve," he said, and he lifted her face to his. Her lips parted, and he kissed her.

It was like the parking lot all over again.

The kiss, the feel of her mouth under his, made his blood pound.

He couldn't remember ever feeling a hunger this deep.

At first, he thought it wasn't the same for her. She didn't move, didn't respond—until suddenly she made a soft little sound in the back of her throat and opened her mouth to his.

Now, he thought.

Right now. Right here. Get this out of the way so he could take her to bed without wondering if he could make it that far, but even in his fevered state, he knew the logistics—the cramped space—made it impossible.

Still, he had to touch her. Intimately.

Her skirt barely covered her thighs and he slid his hand under it, over the warmth of her skin.

She gasped.

"Wait," she whispered, but he couldn't wait, he had to at least do this, God, yes, do this, put his hand between her thighs, lay his palm over her silk thong...

She gave a sweet, breathless cry.

"Travis."

It was the first time she'd spoken his name.

The way she said it, the sudden hot dampness that soaked the thong, almost undid him.

He kissed her again, his tongue sweeping into her mouth. She moaned, dug her hands into his hair and he shoved the thong aside, stroked her, stroked her...

She made high, incoherent little cries.

He could feel his muscles tensing.

If he didn't stop now, it would be too late.

One last quick kiss. Then he stepped from the truck, went

to the passenger side and gathered her into his arms, capturing her mouth with his as he carried her to the private elevator that led to his penthouse.

He set her on her feet, swiped his keycard. The doors opened, then whisked shut, and he clasped her face between his hands.

"Don't be afraid," he said gruffly, though he didn't know what had made him say it. She hadn't been shy about admitting she wanted to go to bed with him.

Still, there was something about her, a hesitancy...

"I'm not afraid," Jennie whispered.

But it was a lie.

Almost as bad a lie as not telling him why she wanted to be with him.

All right.

It wasn't a lie.

What he made her feel had nothing to do with what she'd planned to do tonight.

Well, it did, but not as—as quite a research project.

That was how she'd thought of it from the beginning. That was how she'd intended it, how she'd planned it.

How would he react if he knew that?

More to the point, how would he react if he knew all the rest? If he knew she had never been with a man before...

And almost certainly would never be with one again?

And yet—and yet, all of that had somehow slipped away.

What mattered was how he kissed her, touched her. The way he was kissing her now. The way his erection pressed into her belly.

He felt huge.

Would she be able to—to accommodate him?

She had read scholarly articles, she had seen films. Academic films—sociology majors and psychology majors, grad psych students, often sat through hours of that stuff.

Most people had no idea how graphic those films could be.

But nothing had prepared her for this.

The feel of his aroused sex against her. The promise of all that masculine power. The insistent demand of it.

His mouth was on her breasts now. He nipped lightly at her nipples through the silk of her dress and they hardened into pebbles.

Her breasts ached.

There was an ache low, low in her belly, too.

And she was wet. Wet and hot.

She whimpered as he pushed down the bodice of the dress; his lips closed around one nipple but the silk of her bra was between her flesh and his mouth. The feel of his lips and teeth on her wasn't enough.

It was too much.

How could it be both?

He clasped her shoulders. Turned her, gently so that her back was to him. Her hair had come undone and he nuzzled it aside, kissed the nape of her neck, nipped the flesh, soothed the small, sweet torment with a stroke of his tongue.

She heard the hiss of her zipper.

"Wait," she gasped, "someone might—"

"It's a private elevator," he said in that rough, sexy, gravel-and-velvet whisper. "We're all alone."

Jennie trembled.

All alone, she thought, as her dress slid down her hips and pooled at her feet.

All alone, she thought, as he kissed his way down her spine.

All alone, she thought, as he slowly turned her to him in her black lace bra. Black silk thong. Black, thigh-high stockings. Red stiletto heels.

His gaze moved over her. Slowly, so slowly it made her skin tingle. She felt that tingle in her breasts, her pelvis, her legs.

His eyes lifted. Met hers.

What she saw in those dark depths made her knees go weak.

Her hands came up. One fluttered to her breasts. The other went to the apex of her thighs. Slowly he reached out, caught her wrists, brought her hands to his mouth and kissed the palms.

"Don't hide from me, Genevieve," he said thickly. "Let me see you. You're beautiful. So incredibly beautiful…"

He released one of her wrists. Ran his hand lightly over her, from her lips to throat to her breasts, from her breasts to her belly, her belly to the vee of her thighs, his eyes never leaving hers.

"Travis," she said in an unsteady whisper.

"Yes," he said, "that's right. It's me, touching you. Me, wanting you." His eyes were almost black with hunger as he reached around her, undid her bra, let it drop to the floor. "Beautiful," he whispered, and then his mouth was on her flesh, her breasts, her nipples.

She was coming apart, coming apart, as she sobbed his name again.

"Genevieve. Spread your legs for me."

The words, the way he said them, sent an arrow of longing through her.

"Baby. Spread your legs."

Was it a request? Or was it a command? Either way, it was impossible.

She couldn't. No. She couldn't…

He kissed her again.

Heart pounding, she did what he'd asked.

He said something, low and hot with urgency. She couldn't understand the words but the look on his face told her everything she needed to know.

Still, she wasn't prepared for what happened next, the way he cupped her, the way it felt to know that the heat burning between her legs was now burning his palm.

A high, pealing sob of almost unbearable pleasure broke

from her throat. She swayed. He scooped her into his arms just as the elevator stopped and the doors opened, and she buried her face in the hard curve where his throat and shoulder joined, inhaling the scents of sex, soap and man.

She'd never understood that thing about women liking the smell of male sweat. She knew some of them did, it was a well-researched fact, but it had never made sense until now as she drew the masculine scent of him inside her with every breath.

He carried her through an enormous living room. Light filtered through tall windows, illuminated low furniture, high ceilings, burnished wood floors.

Ahead, a glass and steel staircase angled toward the next level.

He climbed it with her still in his arms, his gait steady, his heart beating against hers. He paused on the landing, kissed her and whispered her name.

Moments later, they were in another enormous room.

His bedroom, with the bed—big, wide, covered with black and white pillows—centered under a star-filled skylight.

He carried her to the bed, stopped beside it and put her down slowly, very slowly, her body sliding against his.

He kissed her.

Sweet, light whispers of his lips on hers that gradually grew deep and hungry until her head was tilted back, her face was raised to his, his hands were deep in the tumble of her hair as he held her.

They were both gasping for air, their breath mingling.

But she was almost naked and he wasn't. It made her feel…

She pulled back.

"What, baby?" he said.

"You haven't—you haven't taken off—"

"No. Not yet." His slow smile raised the temperature a thousand degrees. "I like having you undressed while I'm still wearing my clothes."

The truth was, she liked it, too.

There was something exciting about it.

He kissed her eyes, her mouth. When he swept his fingers over her nipples, she shimmered with heat. When his mouth followed the path his fingers had taken, she moaned.

Why hadn't someone told her this was how it felt, to have a man suck on your breasts? To know that he wanted you and to want him in return with such hot need that it made you breathless?

She heard herself whimper when he drew back.

"It's all right," he whispered, and it was all right because now he was peeling away the narrow strip of silk that secured her thong, working it slowly, slowly down her hips. Her legs.

"Hold on to me," he said gruffly.

She put her hands on his shoulders. He drew the thong to her ankles.

"Lift your foot," he said.

She did.

She would do anything he asked, anything, anything...

Jennie cried out.

But not this!

His mouth, at the delicate curls that guarded her womanhood. His fingers, gently opening her to him. His tongue, licking, teasing...

She wanted to push him away.

Instead, she tangled her fingers in his hair. Her head fell back. She moaned. Something was happening to her. She was trembling. She was coming apart.

The orgasm took her by surprise.

She screamed. Screamed again. Started to fall, but he caught her and took her down to the bed with him.

"Now," she heard herself plead, "please, Travis, please, please, please..."

He tore off his clothes, fumbled open the drawer in the low table beside the bed and took out a foil packet.

She had one quick glimpse of him naked as he tore the packet open.

He was beautiful, all that tanned skin stretched over layers of hard muscle.

And his sex.

She'd been right. He was big. So big.

She felt a moment of trepidation as he rolled the condom on.

"Genevieve."

She blinked, lifted her eyes to his.

He kissed her. Clasped her hands. Brought them high above her head.

And entered her.

At first, she watched his face.

The darkness of his eyes. The tightening of the skin over his cheekbones. The way his lips drew back from his teeth.

Her vision blurred.

She stopped watching.

Started feeling.

And, dear Lord, nothing had ever felt like this.

He was filling her. Moving deeper and deeper into her. She was drowning, drowning in ecstasy, everything in her centered on the feel of him filling her.

Her fingers wove through his.

There was so much of him. Even when she thought she had taken all of him, she hadn't. There was more of him.

More. More.

She gave an inadvertent gasp at a sudden flicker of pain.

He went completely still.

Her eyes flew open. Sweat glistened on his muscled shoulders, his chest, his arms.

"Genevieve?"

She saw the disbelief in his eyes. He was going to stop, she was sure of it, and she couldn't let that happen.

"Genevieve," he groaned, "goddammit, why didn't you—"

She lifted herself to him and impaled herself on his erection.

For a heartbeat, the world stood still.

Then Travis plunged deep, deeper still.

Jennie cried out as a wave of sensation swept her up, lifted her higher than the night, than the stars.

He collapsed against her. She started to put her arms around him but the second she touched him, he jerked away and sat up.

Her throat tightened. Automatically she clutched the duvet to her chin and sat up, too.

"Travis?" She cleared her throat. "Listen, I—I know you didn't expect—"

"Why didn't you tell me?"

"Why would I tell you?" she said in genuine confusion. "It's not exactly a conversation starter."

"I'd have done things differently." He hesitated. "Dammit, I might not have done anything at all. No man wants to be responsible for—for—"

"Is that what's worrying you? It shouldn't. I wanted this to happen. To, you know, lose my, uh, my—"

Ridiculous, that after all of this, she couldn't say the word. But he could.

"Your virginity." He looked at her, his expression unreadable. "Wait a minute. Are you saying you planned this?"

Warning bells rang. Something in the way he'd said that…

Travis grabbed her by the shoulders.

"You did, didn't you?"

She drew her bottom lip between her teeth.

His eyes narrowed.

"So, what was I? The lottery winner?"

"You were—you were a good choice. A very good choice," she said quickly, but she saw his mouth thin.

"A very good choice," he said in a soft, ominous voice.

"Why? Did I meet some kind of criteria? Some—some list of protocols in a textbook?"

"No," she said, and added the first stupid thing that came to mind. "I mean, the protocols I drew up were strictly my own..."

He rolled away, got to his feet.

"Get dressed," he said, his tone not just flat but cold as he grabbed his discarded jeans from the floor and yanked them on.

"Would you just listen to—"

She was talking to an empty room.

Jennie began to shake.

Maybe she hadn't handled this very well but she'd never imagined the man who completed her research would react this way. Weren't men happy to deflower virgins? All the data said they were.

And what did that matter now?

What counted was getting out of here.

She dressed quickly but then, how long could it take to put on a thong and a pair of shoes? Travis Wilde had never gotten around to taking off her stockings.

The very thought sent a rush of humiliation through her bones.

Everything else—her bra, her dress, her purse—was still in the elevator.

She wanted to weep but no way was she going to let that happen.

His shirt was still on the floor.

She snatched it up, dragged it over her head. It fell to the bottom of her buttocks. That left her with the tops of her stockings showing but it would have to do.

She went down the stairs as rapidly as the miserable stiletto heels would permit. The lights were on. She hated their bright luminescence but at least she could see where she was going.

The man who'd taken her virginity was standing at the

far end of the big living room, in front of the open doors of his private elevator. His dark hair was mussed; an overhead spot highlighted the planes and angles of his hard body. He was wearing only his jeans; he'd zipped the fly but he hadn't closed the top button.

He was a gorgeous sight—

As if that mattered.

Her chin came up.

She stalked toward him, hoping she wouldn't ruin her exit by stumbling in the damned shoes.

"Your clothes," he said.

Her face heated. Her dress, her purse, her bra were in the hand he extended toward her. She snatched everything from him, pulled the dress on over the shirt because no way was she going to take it off and let him see her breasts again, and stuffed the bra into her purse, though it barely fit.

She started past him again. His arm shot out and barred her way.

"Excuse me," she said coldly.

"I phoned down. The concierge will have a taxi waiting."

"I can call a taxi by myself."

"Don't be a fool. And take this. It should cover the fare."

She looked at the bills in his hand, then at him.

"I do not want your money, Mr. Wilde."

"Take it."

Jennie shoved his hand aside. "Are you deaf? I said—"

"Did you think this little escapade would be fun? Picking up a stranger. Turning him on. Getting him to take what it's obvious you haven't been able to get rid of in the usual way?"

"I am not going to have this conversation. Just step aside, please."

Travis grabbed her wrist.

"You damned well *are* going to have this conversation! What in hell were you thinking?"

"You want to discuss this?" Jennie said, glaring at him.

"Fine. Let's set the record straight. I did not pick you up. You picked me up."

"Like hell I did ! All I wanted—"

"All you wanted was to use me to save your precious self from getting beaten to a pulp! And I was kind enough to oblige."

"You did a lot more than that, lady."

"You're right. I make the sad mistake of letting you—of letting you seduce me!"

He laughed. Laughed! Jennie balled her hands into fists.

"*I* seduced *you*? You were all over me, baby. What happened tonight was an act of charity on my part. I mean, even without knowing you were a virgin, I knew you were in desperate need of a good—"

Jennie slapped his face.

"You're an unmitigated bastard," she said, her voice trembling.

"And you're a little fool," Travis snarled. "You're just lucky you didn't end up in bed with a—a serial killer!"

"Bad enough I ended up in bed with a—a man who—who doesn't know the first thing about—about sex and how to please a wo—"

Travis hauled her into his arms and kissed her.

She fought. She struggled. He caught her wrists in one hand, dragged her arms behind her and went on kissing her and kissing her until she moaned and her lips clung to his...

That was when he let go of her.

She stared at him, at the arrogant little smile curving his mouth, the I-told-you-so look in his eyes.

She wanted to say something pithy and clever, but her head felt as empty as her heart. The best she could manage was to spin away and stumble into the elevator.

The doors shut.

As soon as they did, she yanked down the straps of her dress, peeled off his T-shirt and dumped it on the floor. Seconds later, she emerged in a marble lobby the size of an airplane hangar. She marched through it, ignored the concierge calling after her, the taxi waiting at the curb. She wanted nothing, absolutely nothing, from Travis Wilde.

It was hotter than blazes, even at this late hour. She walked for endless blocks, sweated through the dress, took off her shoes and carried them because surely women's feet were not meant for four-inch heels.

She knew she must look awful. Cabs slowed when she hailed them, then sped away.

At last, one pulled to the curb.

The driver stared as she climbed in, but she didn't give a damn.

She was heading home, and Travis Wilde was exactly what he'd been intended to be.

An experience.

And if these last months had taught her anything, she thought grimly, as the cab rushed into the night, it was that not all experiences were good ones.

Alone in his condo, Travis paced like a caged tiger.

What kind of woman saw sex as research? What kind of woman thought she could use a man to rid herself of something she no longer wanted, and get away with it?

All those moans when she lay in his arms. The little cries of passion. Part of a plan...

Or real?

Real, judging by the way she'd responded to that last, furious kiss.

Yeah, but so what?

If he hadn't walked over to her in that bar, if someone else had, she'd have ended up in another guy's bed.

His jaw tightened.

And?

What did it matter? Why would he give a crap who Blondie slept with? Who took her virginity?

Who could make her tremble in his arms?

"You're an idiot, Wilde," he snarled.

A furious idiot, and the anger tucked away deep inside him, anger at a world that always seemed determined to prove he was unable to control it despite everything he tried, blazed hot and high.

He wanted to go back to that bar.

He knew the yahoos would be happy to see him, that he and they would step out into the night and trade blows until the darkness receded.

But he was Travis Wilde.

He was a man, not a yahoo. He *was* in control of his life, of himself, of his emotions.

And there was that trip coming up Monday. Not just for himself but for his clients, who had put their trust, and their millions, in his care.

He owed them better, although God only knew what he owed himself.

So he went, instead, to the workout room on the lower level of his penthouse. He ran miles on his treadmill, worked out on the Nautilus, lifted free weights until the sweat poured from his body.

Two hours later, exhausted, he showered, fell into bed and then into a dreamless sleep.

CHAPTER FIVE

TRAVIS'S WEEK PASSED quickly.

Three days in Frankfurt and a last-minute, two-day stop-over in London.

Success in each place, agreements negotiated and concluded. He felt great about it—victory was always sweet—but something was missing.

He couldn't get the woman out of his head.

And it made no sense.

Yes, the sex had been good. Great, when you came down to it. Not because she'd been a virgin but because she'd been—she'd been so sweet. So honest…

Except, she was neither of those things.

Not really.

Sweet? A woman who walked into a bar, looking for a hookup?

Honest? A woman who let a man find out she was a virgin when it was too late to change his mind?

And he would have changed it.

Of course, he would.

A man didn't want the responsibility of taking a woman's innocence…

Her wonderful innocence.

And, hell, what was that all about? He was not, never had

been one of those smug fools who thought a guy was entitled to bed everything in sight, but a woman should live like a nun.

Apparently, Genevieve had.

Until last Friday night.

And then she'd given herself to a man.

To him.

Except, he could have been anybody. That she'd walked into that bar at the right moment had been pure chance.

She hadn't chosen him, she'd stumbled across him.

"Stop it," he muttered, as he sat in the comfort of his private jet, flying high above the Atlantic.

The world was filled with women, beautiful, available women.

What he needed was to call one of them, take her for drinks and dinner.

Good plan.

But it could wait until he was home.

There was no rush.

It was Friday again, they'd land in a few hours, and he could think of half a dozen women who'd drop any plans to spend an evening with him.

Hey, if a man couldn't be honest with himself, who could he be honest with?

Still, he didn't reach for his cell phone when he got to his condo.

He was travel-weary; even the comfort of a private jet didn't make up for things like time zone changes. So he undressed, showered, put on a pair of old gym shorts, opened a chilled Deep Ellum IPA and took it out to the terrace, where he sank down in a lounger.

It was the kind of day Dallas rarely saw in midsummer: warm but not hot, no humidity, the sun shining from the kind of perfect blue sky he'd always associated with home.

Funny.

He'd flown fighters through equally blue skies, under the kiss of an equally hot sun, in places that were just unpronounceable names on a map to most people but those skies, that sun, had always seemed alien, as if he'd gone to sleep at home one night and awakened the next morning in a world that made no sense.

Travis lifted the bottle of ale to his lips and took a long, cooling swallow.

He knew that his brothers, who had also served their country, felt the same.

The wars of the last couple of decades had been very different from the ones their father had talked about when they were growing up.

The old man was a general. Four stars, all rules, regs, spit and polish. He'd raised them on tales of heroism that went back centuries—*"The blood of valiant warriors flows in your veins, gentlemen,"* he'd say—and on stories of their more recent ancestors, men who'd battled their way across the Western plains and settled in what eventually had become Texas, where they'd founded *El Sueño*, the family ranch—if you could call a half a million acre kingdom a "ranch."

Problem was, their father's stories didn't seem to apply to the realities of the twenty-first century, but at least they'd all come home again, if not quite the same way they'd left.

Jake had been wounded in battle, Caleb had been scarred by the dark machinations of an agency nobody talked about.

He'd got off lucky.

No wounds. No scars…

Suddenly he thought back a few years, to a woman he'd dated for a while after he'd come home.

Actually she'd been a shrink with enough initials after her name to fill out the alphabet.

She'd said he had a problem.

He couldn't connect emotionally, she said, and even though she'd sounded angry, she'd sighed and kissed him, and told him she could hear her internal clock ticking and it was time she found a man who wasn't just willing to take risks skydiving and flying and doing who in hell knew what else, it was time to find one ready to risk everything by committing to a relationship.

Travis took another mouthful of ale.

Then she told him she knew he couldn't help it, that he almost surely had PTSD.

But he didn't.

He hadn't bothered telling her that.

After all, she was a shrink and painfully certain that she knew all there was to know about the human psyche but the simple truth was, he'd come through two wars—Afghanistan and Iraq—just fine. No physical injuries, no Post Traumatic Stress Disorder.

A few bad dreams, maybe.

Okay, maybe nightmares, was more like it.

But he'd survive them.

He'd survived nightmares just as bad, the ones that had almost drowned him in despair when he was little and his mother left him.

Travis frowned.

Hell.

She hadn't left him. She'd died. Not her fault. Not anybody's fault. And he'd come through it, gathered himself up, moved on.

One thing a man learned in life.

It wasn't smart to become dependent on another human being.

To get emotionally involved, the way he'd done last week, with Blondie…

"Dammit," he said.

He hadn't gotten involved. Neither had she. Wasn't that the point? That she'd picked him to take her to bed instead of wanting him to do it…

And why was he wasting time, thinking about her? Why was she still in his head at all?

Travis finished the ale, got to his feet and headed inside.

He didn't need a date.

He needed a reality check, and what could be better for that than a couple of hours spent with his brothers?

He made a three-way call, got Jake and Caleb talking. After a couple of minutes of bull, he pointed out that it was Friday night.

"I always told you he was brilliant," Jake said solemnly.

"Yeah," Caleb said. "I bet he even knows the month and the year."

Travis ignored the horseplay.

"So are you two up for it? Can you get away for the evening?"

"Get away?" Caleb snorted. "Of course." And then he must have covered the phone because they heard him say, in a muffled voice, "Honey? You okay with me spending some time tonight with Trav and Jake?"

Travis snickered. Jake didn't. He just said getting together sounded good to him.

"You don't want to check with Addison?" Travis said blandly.

"Why would I?" Jake said, bristling, and then he cleared his throat and said Addison was meeting with her book club tonight anyway, so—

"So," Travis said, reminded once again, as if he needed reminding, of yet another reason why "commitment" was never going to be a word in his vocabulary, "where do you want to meet?"

Jake named a couple of places. Caleb said why didn't they try someplace different? A client had told him good things about a new place that had opened in the Arts District.

"Local beers, good wine list, great steaks, music up front

but booths in the back where, he says, you can actually hear yourself carry on a conversation."

"Won't it be overrun by university types?" Jake said. "You know, alfalfa sprouts, folk music, T-shirts that read, *Schopenhauer Was Right*?"

His brothers chuckled.

"Not if my client likes the place," Caleb said. "His brand of philosophy leans more toward Charlie Brown than Schopenhauer."

They all laughed. Then Jake said, "Okay. Let's try it. Eight? That okay?"

It was perfect, Travis assured them, and he found himself whistling as he headed for the shower.

Jake got there before the others.

He snagged a booth with a crisp fifty dollar bill and when he saw Travis come through the door, he got to his feet and signaled.

"Caleb's client got it wrong," he said. "If it were winter, the amount of tweed in this place would keep us warm straight through until spring."

"Yeah," Travis said, "I noticed. There's some kind of party up front, lots of skinny guys with beards and women with hair under their arms."

Jake laughed. "You always did have a way with words, but what the hell, we're here. And I just saw a platter of rib-eyes go by."

"Always knew you understood the basics," Travis said solemnly. He cocked his head. "Married life agrees with you, buddy. It's made you less ugly, anyway."

Jake grinned and they exchanged quick bear hugs.

"A fine compliment, coming from you, considering everybody says we look like two peas in a pod."

"Three peas," Caleb said, as he joined them. More quick

embraces, a few jabs in the shoulder, and then the brothers slid into the booth.

"How'd the trip to Germany go?"

"Great. I closed one hell of a deal."

"Perfect," Jake told Caleb. "He's handsome, like us. And modest, too. What a guy."

"And your love life?" Caleb said. "How's that going?"

Travis looked at him.

"What's that supposed to mean?"

Caleb raised an eyebrow.

"It means," he said with deliberate care, "how's your love life going?"

"It's going fine."

Jake laughed. "Hey, man. It's not a trick question. Our ladies are certain to ask."

Travis let out a long breath.

"Yeah. Okay. Sorry. I guess I'm still jet-lagged."

"Nobody special yet?"

"No," Travis said evenly. "But you know what I think about this line of questioning?" He sat forward, eyes narrowed. "I think—"

"What *I* think," Caleb said lazily, "is that we'd better decide what we're having, 'cause here comes our waitress."

Their orders were identical.

Porterhouse steaks, baked potatoes with butter, sour cream and chives.

"And an extra-large basket of fried onion rings," Travis said.

"Of course," Jake said, his lips twitching. "Every meal should include a vegetable."

Two beers, an ale for Travis.

The waitress brought those right away, along with a bowl of cashews.

They all dug in, drank, munched, talked about guy stuff. Travis started to relax.

Why had he reacted so negatively to a simple question? It didn't make sense.

Talk helped.

Everyday stuff. Baseball, still going strong. Football, coming up soon. Jake's progress in remodeling the house and sprawling ranch that adjoined *El Sueño*. Caleb and his wife's search for a house and land of their own, and the news that ten thousand acres in Wilde's Crossing had just come on the market.

Their steaks arrived. They ordered more drinks. And just when Travis had almost decided he was home free, his brothers exchanged a look, laid their knives and forks on their plates and Caleb said, "Something bothering you, Trav?"

Travis forced a smile.

"Not a thing. Something bothering *you*, Caleb?"

"Hey," Caleb said lightly, "watch yourself." He waggled his eyebrows. "I'm a trained interrogator, remember?"

Travis laughed, just as he was supposed to do. He thought about playing dumb, tossing back a look of complete innocence and saying he had no idea what they were talking about, but you didn't grow up with two guys who knew everything about you and lie to their faces.

Besides, until this moment, he hadn't realized how much last Friday night—correction, his reaction to last Friday night—was gnawing at him.

Still, he didn't have to tell them all the details.

So he shrugged, put down his knife and fork, too, blotted his mouth with his napkin and said, "I met a woman."

"He met a woman," Caleb said to Jake.

"Wow. Amazing. Our brother, the hotshot hedge fund manager, met a woman. So much for avoiding that question about his love life."

"I didn't avoid anything," Travis said tersely. "This has nothing to with love. And I have nothing to do with hedge funds. I run an investment firm—and why were you talking about me as if I'm not here?"

"Because the last time you were involved with a woman and wouldn't talk about her was when you had that thing going with Suzy Franklin."

Travis sat back, folded his arms over his chest.

"I was in fifth grade. And I wasn't 'involved' any more than I'm 'involved' now."

"He protests too much," Jake said.

"What did I just say about that 'he's not here' routine? And I'm not protesting. There's nothing to protest." He'd meant to make it all sound light but one glance at his brothers and he knew it hadn't worked. He took a breath, let it out and leaned over the table. "Look, it was nothing. See, I was minding my business in this place way downtown…"

"What were you doing downtown?"

"Actually, it was your fault. Your faults. Can you say 'faults'? Because it was. It was last Friday night, you guys couldn't make it, and…"

What the hell.

He told the story.

Most of it.

Some of it.

Finally, he got to the part he was still having trouble with.

"…and," he said, "then the door opened, this woman walked in and she was, ah, she was attractive."

"You mean, she was hot."

A muscle knotted in Travis's jaw.

"You could say that, yeah."

"And?"

"And, I figured if I could convince the drooling yahoos at the bar that I'd been waiting for her to show up, everything would be fine."

"Drooling yahoos," Caleb said dryly.

"What did I say? He has a way with words," Jake said, just as dryly.

"You want to hear this or not?"

"We wouldn't miss it. Go on. A hot babe came strutting through the door—"

"She didn't 'strut,'" Travis said, a little sharply. "And she was—she was good-looking. Not hot. Not the way you're making it…" His words trailed away. His brothers were looking at him as if he'd lost his mind.

Dammit, he thought, and he cleared his throat.

"So, anyway, I, ah, I approached her. I told her I had a problem and asked her for her help. And, after a little, uh, a little persuasion, she agreed."

"Persuasion?"

"What'd you do? Talk her into a coma?"

Travis was silent for a long, long minute. Then he sighed.

"I kissed her," he said in a low voice because, hell, maybe if he talked about it he'd stop thinking about it.

About Genevieve.

Caleb stared at him. "And she went along with it?"

"Yeah."

"Aha." Jacob grinned. "Not just a hot babe. A hot babe looking for a night's diversion."

Travis looked at his brother through narrowed eyes.

"I told you, it's wrong to call her that."

Jake held up his hands. "Okay. Sorry. A lady looking for a night's—"

"She'd walked into the wrong place, that's all," Travis said tightly.

"So, you weren't just looking for her to get you out of there in one piece, you were going to protect her."

"Yes. No. Dammit!" Travis sat back, wrapped his hands around his half-empty mug of ale. "Look, let's drop it, okay? I got into a stupid situation, and that's the end of it."

"Yeah, but I don't see how this played out," Caleb said.

"This jerk and his friends were on you because they figured you'd been hitting on his woman. You said no, you were waiting for your date. This babe—sorry. This woman walked in—"

"She had a name," Travis said, in a dangerously quiet voice. "Genevieve."

Jake waggled his eyebrows. "Wow. Not just good-looking but French."

"Better and better," Caleb said.

Travis opened his mouth, then quickly shut it. All at once he didn't want to talk about last Friday night, not when it would involve giving away details that suddenly seemed far too personal.

"Never mind."

"Never mind? Bro, you can't leave us hanging. We're married men. Happily married, I hasten to add, but still, there's no harm in living vicariously."

"And it was just getting interesting. There you were, in this dive and, wham, a woman walks in, you kiss her, she's warm and willing…and what? You took her home? Went to her place? Or maybe—"

"Enough," Travis snapped.

His tone was cold, hard and flat. His brothers stared at him, then exchanged a quick glance. *What in hell?* that glance said, but they both knew that the line between asking questions and expecting answers had been crossed.

"Right," Jake said, after a few seconds. He cleared his throat. "So, ah, so did I tell you guys about the dude with the fabric samples? Man, I swear, he doesn't speak in any language I ever heard before. Batiste. Bouclé. Brocade. And that's just in the *B*'s…"

Caleb forced a laugh.

Jake kept talking and, finally, Travis forced a laugh, too. The waitress came by. They asked for refills on their drinks, talked some more…

And Travis, who had come out tonight for the express purpose of getting a woman he hardly knew, except in the most basic sense of the word, out of his head now realized he couldn't think about anything except her.

He held up his end of the conversation. More or less. An occasional comment, a laugh when it was expected, but he wasn't really there.

He was in his penthouse, Genevieve in his arms, her responses to his caresses, his kisses, his deep, incredible possession of her so honest, so passionate, so thrilling…until he'd ruined it, ruined everything by reacting like a selfish, stupid kid…

"Travis?"

He wanted to see her again.

Just—just to tell her he'd been wrong, that he shouldn't have said—

"Trav?"

He blinked. Focused his gaze on his brothers. They were staring at him, concern etched into their faces.

"Jet lag," he said with forced good humor. "What I need is coffee. A gallon of it, black and strong and…

His words trailed off.

His heart thudded.

"Travis? You okay?"

The place had gotten crowded with people.

The bunch at the university party up front was still there. If anything, it had grown larger.

Two women, surely from that group, had just walked by. Save-the-Something T-shirts. Real jeans. Leather sandals.

One woman had dark hair.

One had light hair.

The one with the light hair was stumbling. The other was supporting her. Arm around her waist, face a mix of concern and irritation.

"Travis? Man, what's the matter?"

"Nothing," he said, as the women disappeared into the rear bathroom.

It had to be nothing.

The woman who'd been stumbling had looked just like Genevieve. Exactly like her.

Well, not exactly.

Her hair was that same golden color but it wasn't loose, it hung down her back in a long ponytail.

And, of course, she wasn't wearing a dress the size of a handkerchief, or shoes with heels high enough to give a man hot dreams.

So it wasn't her.

It couldn't be her.

It was ridiculous even to think it was her...

The bathroom door swung open. The two women stepped through it.

Travis got to his feet.

"Travis," Caleb said sharply, "what's going on?"

Hell. It *was* her. Genevieve. Her face was drained of color and she had her hand pressed to her belly.

"For crissakes, Gen," the second woman said loudly, "nobody gets sick on two margaritas!"

Travis dug out his wallet, tossed some bills on the table.

"I have to go," he said, his eyes never leaving Genevieve.

"Go where? Dammit, man, talk to us!"

"I'll call you later," Travis said. "Don't worry, everything's fine."

"The hell it is," Jake said.

He started to rise but Caleb, who'd turned to watch Travis, grabbed his arm.

"Let him go."

"Go where? Man, what's happening?"

"Look."

Jake looked.

Travis had reached the women. He said something to them. The one with dark hair gave him a quizzical look.

"You mean, with you?" she said.

Travis's response was loud and clear.

"Absolutely with me," he said, his tone no longer that of a guy who lived for the moment but, instead, that of the tough, take-no-prisoners fighter pilot he'd once been.

"Fine with me," the brunette said. She let go of the blonde, who swayed like a sapling in a Texas dust-storm as Travis scooped her off her feet.

"Whoa," Caleb said.

"Whoa, is right," Jake said, because after a couple of seconds of struggle, the blonde blinked hard, looked up at their brother and said, "Travis?"

"The one and only," Travis said grimly.

She looped her arms around his neck and buried her face against his throat. And he, jaw set, eyes hard as obsidian, carried her straight through the room and out the door.

CHAPTER SIX

TRAVIS WAS DRIVING his 'Vette tonight, not his truck. He'd parked it a short way down the street.

He hadn't thought about it, one way or the other—until he walked out of the bar with Genevieve in his arms.

Now he figured that having to walk a couple of minutes to get to the car was probably a good thing.

It would give him time to cool down.

He was beyond angry.

What in hell was in this woman's head?

Didn't she have any sense of reason? Walking into that bar last week, dressed to raise the blood pressure of every man breathing, and now, this. Drinking herself damned near senseless.

He didn't like rules, didn't believe in worrying much over what social pundits liked or disliked, but he did have opinions—and one of them was that a woman out of control was not a pretty sight.

As for drunks…

He didn't like drunks in general but when a woman went that route…

His sisters would say he was being sexist. Maybe he was, but that was how he felt.

And what if Genevieve hadn't got sick? What would have come next? Would she have let some guy pick her up, take her home? Touch her? Kiss her? Ease her thighs apart, bury himself in all that honeyed sweetness?

So much for calming down. If anything, his anger ratcheted up a notch.

A couple walking toward them laughed.

"Very romantic," the woman said.

Travis glowered. If only they knew the truth. This was as far from "romantic" as a man could get—and it was stupid.

What he was doing was stupid.

He wasn't Genevieve's keeper.

He should have left her with her pals. She was their problem, not his.

It wasn't too late; he could turn around, take her back to where he'd found her…

Genevieve moaned softly.

Yeah, but she was sick. Drunk, sure. But sick drunk made for a dangerous situation.

Two margaritas, her friend had said.

Hardly enough to get sick on, but she was. The moans. The way she'd clutched her belly. Even the way she'd let him all but kidnap her said everything he needed to know.

She was sick. And she needed—

She needed him.

He'd known it when he heard her whisper his name, when she gave herself over to him, buried her face against his throat.

She felt soft and feminine in his arms. And that sense that she trusted him. Needed him…

He tried not to think about that, or the way it made him feel.

It was a lot safer to concentrate on his anger.

"Damned fool woman," he muttered.

"I'm sorry," she said in a shaky whisper.

He hadn't meant her to hear him, but maybe it was a good thing that she had.

"Yeah," he said coldly, "right. I'm sure you are. Somebody

should have told you that what comes after the booze is never as much fun as the partying that precedes it.

She shook her head. Her hair slipped like silk across his jaw.

"I meant that I'm sorry for this. Not your problem."

"Damned right," he growled.

Jennie expected nothing more.

She knew he wouldn't say she didn't have to apologize, that he was only glad he'd been there to help her…

Genevieve Cooper, are you truly crazy?

It was her alter-ego talking, but Jennie refused to listen. She wasn't Genevieve, not anymore.

Plus, she knew what Travis Wilde was like. Hadn't she learned all she needed to know last week?

Besides, he had every right to be harsh and judgmental. He thought she was drunk. How could he possibly know the truth, that what she really was, was incredibly stupid?

No alcohol with these pills, Jennifer, the doctor had said.

Sure. But what did doctors know? Not much, as the last months had surely proved.

But the righteous Travis Wilde had no way of knowing that, and she wasn't about to enlighten him.

She'd decided, from the beginning, to keep her own counsel, which was a fancy way of saying it was her life and what was happening to her was her business, and she didn't want anybody involved in it.

Her parents were gone. She had no brothers or sisters. The last thing she wanted were strangers, offering phony sympathy. She'd had her fill of that from well-meaning hospital volunteers. Or therapy groups, where everybody thought they had problems until they heard hers.

She'd even tried private counseling, and what a joke that had become when the shrink had broken protocol, reached out and hugged her.

Protocol.

There it was again, the same stupid word that had fallen from her lips last week, after a simple decision to—to take her research to another level had led her into this man's arms, into letting herself feel like a woman instead of a—a creature drowning in a sea of test tubes and lab notes.

And what a mistake that had turned out to be.

Her car was just ahead. Thank goodness. Another minute and she would never have to see Travis Wilde again.

Jennie gathered all her strength, told herself it was vital that she not sound as awful as she felt.

"The tan Civic," she said. "It's mine." He didn't answer, didn't even slow down. "Mr. Wilde. I said, that tan car…"

"I heard you."

"Then put me—"

"You can get it tomorrow, when you're up to driving."

"I have already had the pleasure of retrieving my car, thanks to you. I have no intention of doing it again."

"I don't think you want to argue over the reasons you had to leave your car, last week or this."

He was right. She didn't. What she had to do was exert control.

"I am perfectly capable of driving my own car."

Sick as she was, she was pleased to have achieved what she thought was a determined tone.

Perhaps not.

He laughed, though it was not a pretty sound.

"And pigs can fly." He set her on her feet, held her steady with one arm around her waist while he dug out his keys and opened the 'Vette's door. "Get in."

"Where's Brenda? Brenda can—"

"Brenda's still partying with the rest of your pals. Go on. Get in."

"No. I absolutely refuse to have you—"

He muttered something short and graphic, scooped her

up again and put her into the passenger seat. Then he closed the door, went to the driver's side and got behind the wheel.

"Seat belt," he said sharply.

"Really, I don't—"

He reached across her, grabbed the end of belt and brought it over her body. His hand brushed over her breasts. She thought of what it would be like if he really touched her, not in passion but in an offer of comfort.

"Comfort" was not in his game plan.

She could tell by the way he fastened the latch, his motions brisk and efficient.

"What's your address?"

"I don't need your help, Mr. Wilde."

"Yes," he snarled, "you do. And it's a little late for formality, isn't it? I wasn't 'Mr. Wilde' when you were in my bed."

A wave of hot color rose in her face.

Nice, Travis told himself, a truly nice touch. She didn't deserve to be coddled but she was sick and he'd taken it upon himself to see her safely home.

Besides, he had no right to judge her.

She'd walked into a bar, looking for a hookup?

Her business, not his.

She drank to excess?

Her business again, absolutely not his.

There wasn't any reason to make things worse than they already were, especially when his real anger had just reversed itself and gone from her as its target to himself.

Touching her breasts had been inadvertent.

And his body had not clenched with desire.

Desire, even with her like this, he would have understood. What he'd felt instead, the overwhelming need to take her in his arms and comfort her, was the last thing he'd expected.

He didn't understand it.

Didn't want to understand it.

What he wanted to do was get her to her apartment and then get the hell out of her life.

Whatever life that was.

Who was this woman? Everything about her confused him, even the way she looked…Entirely different than last week.

Far as he could tell, she didn't have a touch of makeup on her face. Her hair was pulled back. She had on a cotton blouse. Sleeveless, simple, buttons all the way down the front. It was tan, pretty much the same color as her box-on-wheels automobile. And she was wearing jeans. Plain, no-name denim, not the torn kind that cost hundreds of bucks just so the wearer could look like somebody who actually worked for a living. Her feet were encased in flat leather sandals.

Nothing with the kind of heel that made a man play sexual fantasies in his head.

Not that she needed to dress the part of temptress.

She was beautiful just as she was, and even knowing she seemed woefully short on logic and maybe on morals didn't change the fact that he still wanted to hold her close and tell her he'd take care of her…

He hated himself for it.

Jaw set, he fastened his seat belt and started the engine. The Corvette roared to life.

"I'm still waiting for you to tell me where you live."

"This is ridiculous." She reached for the door handle. "I'll go back and get Brenda. She can—"

"No. She can't. I'm driving you home and it's not up for discussion. Now, what's your address?"

Jennie closed her eyes.

If only she hadn't let Brenda talk her into going out with most of the department to celebrate Peter Haley finally nailing his doctorate.

"Come on," Brenda had said. "You've been mopey all week. A couple of hours away from the books will make you feel better."

Maybe it would, she'd thought. So she'd gone with them.

And she hadn't even ordered the margarita.

Peter had, and everybody had looked at her when it arrived.

She knew why. It was because she never drank, not even that staple of university life—beer.

Don't you drink, Jen? someone always said. Or, *Good for you! I've heard that these 12 step programs are hard to stick with.*

Either way, there was no good rejoinder.

She was tired of people looking at her, of always being the one who ordered a Diet Coke.

One sip of the pale blue margarita, she'd thought. What harm could one sip do?

It had tasted lovely.

And it had *felt* lovely. Not the alcohol. What had been lovely was that, for the first time in months, she felt normal.

To hell with it, she'd thought, and she'd gulped down half of it—half, not two full drinks as Brenda had claimed.

And yes, for a couple of minutes she'd felt good.

And she was desperate to feel good.

To stop thinking about what lay ahead, and what it would be like.

To stop thinking about last week, and how she'd made a fool of herself with this very man.

This man who was every bit as gorgeous and as arrogant as she'd remembered.

The truth was, she remembered too much.

The feel of his hands on her. The way he kissed. And wasn't that pitiful? That all of that should still be with her? That a man who was such an unmitigated bastard could be such an accomplished lover that a week later, despite the fact that she despised him, that she couldn't afford to waste precious time on such nonsensical stuff, the sight of him could still make her heart start to race?

If only he hadn't been in the bar tonight…

"Are we going to sit here all night?" her unwanted rescuer said. "Because we will, unless you give me your address."

He would do it, Jennie knew. The best thing to do was give in, let him drive her home and know she would never have to deal with him again.

"I live near the university," she said in weary resignation. "Farrier Drive. It's a couple of miles past—"

"I can find it," he said.

She had no doubt that he could.

Besides, she had other things to think about.

Like not throwing up again, until she was alone—but, oh, dear God, that wasn't going to work out...

"Stop the car," she gasped.

He glanced at her, then swerved across two lanes of traffic to the curb. She had barely undone her seat belt when he was out of the car and at her side.

"Easy," he said, as he helped her onto the sidewalk.

A cramp pinched her belly and she groaned, leaned over and vomited although the truth was, mostly, she just gagged and made terrible sounds because there was really nothing left in her belly, but that didn't make things any less horrible, especially because Travis Wilde, world-class rat, stood behind her as if he weren't a rat at all, holding her shoulders and steadying her.

Done, she trembled like a leaf.

"Don't move," he said in a low voice.

She felt him lift one hand from her, then the other, as he slipped off his dark gray sports jacket, then wrapped it around her.

She wanted to tell him she didn't need it—it had to be ninety degrees tonight—but the truth was, she was ice-cold.

"Thank you," she said in a choked whisper.

He turned her toward him, took a pristine white handkerchief from his pocket. She reached for it, but she was shaking too hard to grasp it.

"Let me," he said.

She could hardly meet his eyes as he gently wiped her mouth, afraid of the censure she'd see in his gaze.

"Hey," he said softly. He put his fingers under her chin and raised her face to his, and what she saw in his eyes was compassion.

It made her want to lean forward and rest her head against his chest, but she knew better than to do that.

He was being kind. Not what she'd expected from him. And the last thing she needed. Too much kindness and she'd fall apart.

"I'm—I'm okay."

He nodded. "You will be. Getting all that booze out of your system helps."

"It isn't the tequila," she heard herself say, and could have bitten off her tongue, but he didn't pick up on it.

Instead, he smiled.

"It never is. And if it makes you feel any better, I'm not a novice at this. Heck, I have three sisters, all younger than I am, and I remember helping them clean up after a party."

It wasn't true.

He'd never had to do anything like that for Em or Lissa or Jaimie. If they'd gotten themselves plastered—and now that he thought about it, he figured the odds were good they each must have, at least once in their teen years—they'd covered for each other.

He, Jake and Caleb had covered for each other, too.

Genevieve had nobody to turn to.

Nobody but him.

The thought put a little twist in his gut.

Her face was pale; the elastic thing, whatever women called it, around her ponytail had come loose and strands of pale blond hair were in her eyes.

He tucked the strands behind her ears.

"Okay now?" he said quietly.

She nodded.

He steadied her with one hand, reached into the 'Vette, opened the console, took out a small bottle of water. He opened it; she held out her hand but she was still trembling.

"Here," he said, bringing the bottle to her lips.

She tilted her head back. Drank. Rinsed her mouth, then spat out the water.

"Thank you."

"Finish it."

"I really don't want—"

"Water will make you feel better."

He tilted the bottle to her lips again; she put her hand over his so she could lift it higher. His skin was warm, the feel of his fingers under hers reassuring.

"Good girl," he said, and she, a lifelong advocate for women's rights, felt herself glow under the words of what any self-respecting feminist would call sexist praise.

He capped the empty bottle, tossed it into the back of the car.

"Want to stay here, get a little more fresh air?"

"No. I feel much better."

"Are you sure?"

She couldn't bear the way he was looking at her, his eyes warm not only with compassion but with sympathy. She couldn't tolerate anything close to pity; it was the reason she'd left New England and come here, where nobody knew her.

And now there was this man who had suddenly turned sweet and generous and kind...

"I'm sure." She stood a little straighter. "Look, I know you're afraid I'm going to get sick in your car—"

"I'm not worried about the car."

"Of course you are. Why else would you give a damn?"

Good. That cold glare was in his eye again.

"You have one hell of an opinion of me."

"It only matches your opinion of me."

He opened his mouth, closed it again.

"Okay," he said, after a minute, "how about a truce?"

Her eyes met his. She shrugged.

"Fine."

He smiled. "Lots of enthusiasm in that word, Genevieve."

She stood straighter.

"My name isn't Genevieve." She took a deep breath. What did it matter what he called her? And yet, somehow, it did. "My name is Jennifer. Jennie."

He raised one dark eyebrow. "Why the pseudonym?"

"It wasn't a pseudonym."

The corner of his lips twitched.

"What else would you call using a phony name?"

She considered not answering, but she owed him some kind of honesty, even if it was only the smallest bit.

"I used a different name because—because that wasn't me last Friday night, okay? That—that creature who got all dressed up and headed into that bar. I wasn't that woman who—who went home with a strange man and—and—"

She felt her eyes fill with tears, and wasn't that pathetic? She looked away from him, or would have, but he caught her face in his hands and wiped away her tears with his thumbs.

"You weren't a creature. You were a beautiful woman. Brave, too."

His voice was soft. She didn't want softness, dammit. She wanted him to be the callous bastard she'd pegged him for.

She didn't want to like him.

She didn't want to need him.

She couldn't need anybody.

Not now. Not ever. Not—

"Baby," he said, not just softly but gently. It was too much, and she had to deal with it.

"And my name certainly isn't 'baby,' either." She jerked free of his hands. "So if you think a—a ration of Texas sweet-talk is going to make me dumb enough to sleep with you again—"

He let go of her, fast. So much for declaring a truce.

"Your mama should have taught you that it's polite to wait until you're asked." His eyes narrowed to icy slits. "Do us both a favor, *Genevieve*. Get back in the car so I can take you home and know we'll never have the misfortune to see each other again."

His comment had been no nastier than hers, but it hurt. She wanted to zing back a clever response, then walk away, but her brain was foggy, they were miles from her apartment—and she knew damned well that on this particular night, walking home wasn't an option.

"An excellent plan, Mr. Wilde," she said coldly. "And thanks again for reminding me that you are, indeed, a callous, pluperfect rat."

It wasn't much, but it was the best she could do.

She swung away. A sharp pain lanced through her head; the earth tilted. She gave it a couple of seconds until things steadied. Then she got into the car.

He got in on his side, slammed the door hard enough to make her jump.

The car flew into the night, and Jennie prayed that the pain in her head wouldn't get so bad that it would make her weep.

Neither of them said anything more until Travis turned onto her street, and into the garden apartment complex in which she lived.

The pain in her head had eased off. A minor miracle, but it wouldn't last. She needed to take a pill before it returned.

"Which building?" he said.

"You can stop at the corner."

"I can stop in front of your door. Which building?"

"You don't have to—"

"You're right, I don't. But I will. For the last time, which building?"

God, he was impossible. Maybe some women liked to be bossed around but she wasn't one of them. Still, if it got her home faster…

"That one," she said. "At the corner."

He drove to the end of the block, then into the driveway that led behind the building.

"What are you doing?"

He didn't answer but then, he didn't have to. What he was doing was obvious.

He was pulling into a slot in the small parking area.

"I'm seeing you to your door," he said brusquely.

"That is absolutely not—"

She was talking to the air. He was out of the car, already opening her door.

Jennie rolled her eyes and stepped outside.

"Do you always ignore people's wishes, Mr. Wilde?"

"Only when their wishes don't make sense, Miss…?"

"Cooper," she snapped.

"Only when their wishes don't make sense, Miss Cooper. Twenty minutes ago, you were tossing your cookies."

"That's a horrible phrase!"

"It isn't as bad as the act itself."

They were walking toward the back entrance to her two-story building. He tried to take her arm; she shook him off.

It was a stupid thing to do, considering that it was dark—one of the lights over the door had burned out—and the lot had potholes big enough to swallow you whole.

Inevitably she stumbled.

Just as inevitably, he caught her, put his arm around her waist.

"I don't need—"

"I'll be the judge of that."

"Dammit, Wilde—"

"Great," he said tightly. "No more 'mister.' At least we'll be on a less formal basis before you go facedown out here."

"I hate to spoil that lovely image but it won't happen. I'm much better now, thank you very much, and you've brought me to my door, so—"

"Keys."

"What is wrong with you? I just said—"

"I'm taking you to your apartment. Keys."

He held out his free hand, snapped his fingers—and was rewarded with the sight of her chin lifting and her eyes narrowing.

Damned if she didn't look like she wanted to slug him.

He fought against a smile.

No matter what, you had to admire her spirit. All dressed up for a night on the town, dressed down for a night with friends, sick or not, Jennie Cooper was one interesting woman.

She held the keys up by two fingers, gave him a four-letter smile and dropped them in his palm.

This time, what he fought back was a burst of laughter.

She had more than spirit; she had resiliency.

For some crazy reason, he wanted to kiss her, and that was patently ridiculous. Instead he did the only safe thing: turned his back to her and unlocked the door.

It opened on the kind of hallway he suspected was endemic to cheap student housing everywhere. A narrow corridor, dim lighting, closed doors.

Nothing unusual.

Still, a caution born of years spent on not-necessarily-friendly territory half a world away made him move forward and enter the hall first. A quick but efficient glance revealed nothing more threatening than a moth batting against an overhead light at the foot of a staircase.

He turned, ready to signal her past him, but she was already moving.

Her body brushed his.

His breath nearly stopped. And unless he'd forgotten how to read women, so did hers.

Electricity filled the space between them.

He knew what he wanted to do.

Take Jennie in his arms. Kiss her. Touch her. She'd let him do it, too. He knew it as surely as he knew what that look in her eyes meant...

How many bad ideas could a man have in one night?

He took a step back.

"Okay," he said briskly. "Which apartment?"

He wanted her to say it was on the second floor. Then he'd have the excuse to hold her in his arms again, but she swallowed hard, dragged her gaze from his and nodded toward the nearest door.

They walked to it. The same key opened the door, and they stepped inside.

The place was like all the off-campus housing complexes he'd visited back in his university days.

Small. Institutionally-furnished. Nothing to define it as Jennie's, except for a small plush animal sitting in a corner of the sofa.

It was a dog with long, floppy ears. One long, floppy ear, anyway. The other was pretty much gone, as was most of a faded red bow around its neck.

It was the kind of sentimental keepsake his sisters—well, Emily, anyway—were big on. Somehow, he hadn't expected Jennie to harbor such attachments.

"A silly thing."

Travis turned around. Jennie was standing a few feet away, eyes fixed on him.

"The dog," she said. "I don't know why I keep it."

"It's not silly to keep something you love."

"I don't love it. Why would anybody love a beat-up old toy?"

Their eyes met.

She cleared her throat.

"I need to—to—"

She gestured toward what he figured was the bathroom.

"Yes. Sure." He cleared his throat. "I'll wait."

"No. I mean, you don't have to…"

"I'll wait," he said.

She nodded.

Safely inside the bathroom, the door closed and locked, Jennie stared at herself in the mirror.

She looked awful.

Not that it mattered.

Travis had performed a rescue mission; what she looked like was unimportant.

She peed. Washed her face. Brushed her teeth. Took a pill for her headache, just in case it returned.

Then she took a few deep breaths, let them out, opened the door and went back into the living room.

He was standing beside the window.

Say something, she told herself, say anything!

"Great view of the parking lot, huh?" she said briskly.

He turned around.

"Yeah." A quick smile. "Well. Are you going to be okay?"

"I'll be fine."

"Because if you still feel sick—"

"Travis? What I said before, about it not being the tequila… It's the truth. I—I wasn't drunk."

She spoke the words in a rush, even as she chastised herself for having said them.

"Look, I didn't mean to…I shouldn't have set myself up as judge and jury. You drank too much. So what? Believe me, I've done the same—"

"It was a reaction to medication."

"Medication?"

He looked startled. Jennie's heart thudded. He couldn't

be more startled than she was but somehow, it had become important that he not think worse of her than he already did.

"You mean, an allergic thing?"

She took a deep breath.

"Not exactly. I get—I get headaches." That was certainly true enough. "I take something for them and—and the doctor warned me it wouldn't mix well with liquor but—but—"

"But, you forgot."

She hadn't forgotten. She'd just thought, *What the hell is the difference?*

Life was closing down so quickly…

But she couldn't tell him that.

"Something like that," she said, trying for a carefree smile.

He smiled, too. Her heartbeat quickened. She'd almost forgotten how devastating his smile was: charming, flirtatious, sexy…and all Travis Wilde.

"Well," he said, "after what happened tonight, you won't forget next time."

They both laughed politely—but nothing in their eyes was polite. The way he was looking at her, the way she was looking at him…

She turned away and walked to the door.

He followed.

She looked at him, held out her hand. He took it.

His touch sent a wave of longing through her.

"Anyway—anyway, thanks for taking me home."

"No," he said, "thank *you*."

"For what?"

"For tolerating me being such an ass."

"You weren't. I mean, you had every reason to think I was just plain drunk."

"Even so, I had no right to judge you." His hand tightened around hers; he moved closer. "As for last week—"

"Really," she said quickly, "there's no need to—"

"There's every need. You gave me a gift beyond measure that night."

She felt her face flame with color.

"No. I understand. I burdened you with—"

"You *honored* me." His voice was rough, so sexy she could hardly breathe. "No woman's ever given me such an incredible gift before."

He meant it. She could see it in his eyes, hear it in his words. It made her want to explain…at least, to explain as much as she could.

"Travis," she said softly, "I know I made it sound as if—as if you—as if what we did—was just something that I'd planned could happen with anybody. But—but—"

"But what?"

The rest was hard to say. To admit. She didn't want to embarrass him. Or embarrass herself. But he had the right to hear it.

She took a deep breath.

"But one step inside that bar and I knew I'd never go through with it. And then—and then—"

His eyes darkened.

"And then?"

"And then I saw you."

"You were a miracle, coming through that door," he said softly. "I told myself the miracle was that you could save my sorry tail…" He cupped her face with his hands. "But the truth is, the miracle was that you were so beautiful. And that I wanted you the second I saw you."

Her smile, her sigh, told him everything he'd spent the past week needing to know.

"Truly?" she said, all the innocence in the world in the one, softly-spoken word.

"Truly," he said. "I never wanted a woman the way I wanted you."

"What we did," she whispered, "it was—it was—"

"Incredible," he whispered back, putting his arms around her, bending his head to hers, nuzzling her hair away from her temple. "I thought about you every single minute since that night."

"Did you?" she said, her voice trembling.

"Every waking moment." He smiled. "Every sleeping moment, too." His smile tilted. "I dreamed about you."

Was he saying that to make her feel better, or did he mean it?

Stop analyzing, was the last thing her alter-ego said, before she sent it packing and moved fully into his embrace.

She could feel the hard, quick race of his heart.

"I—I dreamed about you, too."

He cupped her face. Lifted it to his.

"I don't want to leave you," he said gruffly.

Jennie took a deep, deep breath.

"Then don't," she whispered.

Travis kissed her. She kissed him back. He groaned, kissed her again, hard and deep.

Then he reached past her, and closed the door.

CHAPTER SEVEN

HE WASN'T GOING to make love to her.

What kind of man took advantage of a woman when she didn't feel well?

He just—he just wanted to hold her.

Be with her.

Kiss her, just a little. Like this. God, yes, like this. Kisses that made her tremble in his arms.

And he wanted to touch her.

Not in a way that demanded anything of her. Asked anything of her.

He only wanted to feel the softness of her hair as it slid through his fingers, the warmth of her skin under the stroke of his hand.

But with her lips clinging to his, parting to his, with her body pressed to his, wanting was rapidly giving way to the heady rush of need.

For the first time in his life, Travis saw the difference between the two.

He was a man who prided himself on self-control, even in sex. Especially in sex. Only a fool let his emotions carry him away with a woman.

But it was different with her.

With Jennie.

He couldn't get his thoughts together. Couldn't focus on anything but her taste, her heat, her sweet moans.

He tried.

He clasped her shoulders. Drew back, just a little. Looked down into her lovely, innocent face.

"Honey." His voice was hoarse; he cleared his throat but it didn't help. "Jennie. We don't have to do anything more than—"

She rose to him, put her hands into his hair, silenced him with a kiss.

"Are you telling me you don't want me?" she whispered.

Travis took her hand, placed it over his racing heart, then brought it down, down, down to the fullness straining the fabric of his fly.

"What do you think?" he said thickly.

She gave a soft, incredibly sexy laugh.

"I think you need to take me into the bedroom. Behind you, through that door."

He lifted her into his arms, carried her into a room that was hardly big enough to contain a chest of drawers. A nightstand.

And twin beds.

He almost laughed. Whatever he'd expected, it hadn't been this.

"It could be worse," Jennie said, as if she knew what he was thinking. He looked down at her, saw that her lips were curved. "The bedroom in my last place had bunk beds."

He did laugh, then; she did, too. But when he felt the brush of her breasts and belly against him as he lowered her slowly to her feet, their laughter faded.

Her eyes were filled with need.

Filled with him.

Desire, sharp and hot, still burned within him.

But so was something else.

He wanted to—to take care of her. Protect her.

He wanted to be the lover he had not been that first time. The lover she deserved.

He kissed her. Gently. Framed her face with his big hands.

"I'm going to undress you," he said softly. "And lie down with you in my arms. We don't have to do anything more than that tonight."

When she parted her lips to answer him, he silenced her with a kiss.

Then, slowly, his eyes fixed to hers, he began undoing the buttons of her blouse.

Normally, he was fine with buttons. Small, round bits of plastic; how difficult could opening them be, especially for a guy who'd been undressing women since the age of sixteen?

Very difficult.

His fingers seemed too big. Clumsy. He found himself concentrating, hard, on every miserable one of what seemed like an endless line of tiny plastic rounds that marched down her blouse.

She made a little sound.

He looked up.

"What?" he said, a little gruffly.

"Nothing. I mean—I mean—I can't—" Her hands closed over his. "Tear the blouse, if you have to. Just—just touch me…"

On a deep, long groan, he did what she'd asked and tore the delicate fabric in two.

Then he drew back.

Not a lot. Just enough so that his eyes could take delight from the delicate beauty he'd uncovered.

Creamy shoulders. The rise of rounded breasts above a simple, white cotton bra. A tiny, heart-shaped birthmark just below the hollow of her throat.

How could he not have noticed that last time?

How could he not have noticed how sweet, how innocent she was?

He kissed the heart.

Kissed the delicate curve of flesh rising above the bra.

Kissed the center of each cup, where the faint pucker of fabric hinted at the nipples that awaited the touch of his tongue.

Jennie made a sound that tore straight through him.

"Travis," she whispered, and he knew that no one had ever said his name with as much tenderness.

He reached for the clasp on her jeans.

Undid it.

Took hold of the zipper tab.

Drew it down.

Slowly he eased the jeans down her legs.

Such long, endless legs.

She was trembling.

Hell, so was he.

He slipped off her shoes, one at a time. Looked at her. Like this, barefoot, wearing the simplest bra and panties, she was a woman a man would ache to possess.

And, God, yes, he ached. For her.

"You're beautiful," he said softly.

Color swept into her face.

"I want to be," she said. "For you."

That was what he wanted, too. That her beauty, her unique self, be only for him.

"Aren't you—aren't you going to touch me?"

Her words were a magnificent torment. He wanted to do exactly that, wanted it more than anything…

He was drawn as tight as a bow.

He could see the pulse beating just beneath the tiny heart-shaped birthmark.

"Is that what you want?"

"Yes. Oh, yes."

"Take my hand," he said in a gravel-rough voice. "Show me where you want me to touch you."

He held his hand out to her. She stared at it. At him. He forced himself not to move.

It seemed an eternity but, at last, she took his hand. Brought it to her cheek. To her throat.

Her lips.

Parted them, and sucked one of his fingers into her mouth.

A low moan rose in his throat.

He was going to come. Sweet Lord, he was going to come...

He drew a harsh breath. Focused on her. Felt the pounding in his veins ease.

"Where else shall I touch you?" he said in a choked whisper.

Her eyes locked with his. She brought his hand down her throat.

To her breast.

Travis closed his eyes. Cupped his hand around the sweet weight, felt the push of the cotton-covered nipple into his palm.

"And—and here," she whispered, as she drew his hand over her ribs, over her belly...

And stopped.

She couldn't go any farther.

What she was doing was beyond anything she'd ever imagined doing with a man.

Letting him touch her so intimately.

Guiding his hand over her body.

Watching his face as she did it, seeing his tanned skin seem to tighten over the bones beneath it.

"Jennie."

She blinked.

His eyes had narrowed and glittered like shards of obsidian in the night.

"Don't stop," he said. "Show me what you want."

She took a breath. Took another.

"I want your hand here," she whispered, and she shifted her weight, brought his palm between her thighs, placed it against the part of her that throbbed with need for him.

He said something, low and fierce and shockingly primal.

She was hot and wet, and he couldn't wait, couldn't hold back, couldn't…

"Travis," she sobbed, "please, please…"

He reached for his jacket, prayed there were some forgotten condoms in the interior pocket. Yes. Thank God, there were two slim packets.

"Jennie," he whispered, "beautiful Jennie."

Somehow, he tore off his clothes. Fumbled with her bra, got the clasp undone, tried to deal with her panties, cursed and, instead, ripped them from her.

She was moving against him, her body hot against his, her mouth open and wet and seeking on his.

All his thoughts about doing this slowly, gently, never mind maybe not doing it at all, vanished like smoke on a windy morning.

The bed was a million miles away.

The wall was much closer.

"Hold on to me," he said as he lifted her. "Your arms around my neck. Your legs around my waist…"

She screamed his name as he thrust into her.

He went still; was he hurting her?

"Don't stop," she said, "don't-stop-don't-stop-don't-stop—"

He took her mouth with his. And moved inside her. Hard. Fast. She screamed as she came and still he went deeper, deeper, so deep that when the triumphal cry of his completion escaped his throat, the world spun away.

* * *

Somehow, they made it to the bed.

He put her down, kissed her, found his way to the bathroom and disposed of the condom.

The mattress was narrow; she made room for him but he gathered her to him, held her so she was draped over him, and the fact that there wasn't really room for two people in her bed didn't matter because he was never going to let go of her.

He was going to hold her like this until the end of time.

"Travis."

"Mmm?"

"I'm too heavy…"

He laughed.

So did Jennie.

It was a lovely feeling, all that rock-hard male muscle vibrating with laughter beneath her.

The scientist in her had never thought that people would laugh when they made love.

The woman in her was thrilled by the realization.

"Seriously. You can't be comforta—"

"You know," he said, "when I was a kid, I had this old blanket that I absolutely adored."

She folded her hands on his chest, propped her chin on them and gave him a wary look.

"And?"

"And," he said, his expression dead-serious, "I couldn't go to sleep unless I had it draped on top of me."

It took all her effort to keep a straight face.

"Nice. Very nice. So, I remind you of an old blanket?"

He grinned.

"Does it help if I say it was a comforter, not a blanket?"

Jennie sank her teeth lightly into his shoulder. He gave a mock yelp.

"Hey. That was a compliment."

"Telling a woman she reminds you of a blanket, even if you call it a comforter, is *not* a compliment, Mr. Wilde."

"I didn't tell it to a woman, I told it to you." His grin faded. "Only to you, Jennie. Because you're the only woman I want in my arms."

"That's lovely," she said softly. "Because you're the only man I want in mine."

He kissed her. Kissed her again. She could feel him hardening against her and then he kissed her one last time and gently moved out from under her.

"Don't go," she said, before she could call back the plea, but it was okay, saying it, letting him know how much she wanted him, it was fine because he kissed her again and told her, against her lips, that he wasn't going anywhere except to get another condom.

"Why would I ever leave you?" he said when he came back to her and rolled her beneath him.

"Travis." His name trembled on her lips. "Oh, Travis…"

"Jennie," he whispered, and then he was inside her.

She awoke to middle-of-the-night darkness, and to confusion.

She was in her bed—there was no mistaking the lumpy mattress—but she wasn't alone.

She was lying on her side, head pillowed on a hard shoulder. An equally hard arm and leg were flung possessively over her body.

For a split second, her brain froze.

And then it all came back.

Travis, taking her out of that bar. His anger and then his concern. His toughness and then his tenderness.

His lovemaking.

His amazing, incredible, glorious lovemaking.

I should get up, she thought. *Do whatever it is a woman does when she awakens with a man beside her.*

What *did* you do in those circumstances?

You left the bed. And, what? Did you do just the basics? A bathroom visit? Fix your hair? Put on some makeup? Get dressed. Oh, absolutely. Get dressed, for sure. Get out of the bedroom, give the man some space.

All of that made sense.

Except, she really didn't want to move.

It was—well, it was lovely, just lying here, Travis's shoulder serving as her pillow, his arm and leg over her.

He was so warm. So solid.

So wonderfully real.

Sex wasn't what you read about in textbooks. It wasn't what you saw in psych counseling videos. It was—it was—

It was Travis.

He stirred in his sleep; his arm tightened around her and he drew her closer.

And this. Waking in a man's arms. The feeling of him caring about you, protecting you.

Who would have dreamed that, too, was part of sex?

Research. That was what she'd called her plan to learn what sex was like, because calling it anything else had seemed ugly—but there was no pretending this was research any longer.

This was about him. Travis Wilde. A man she'd picked up in a bar, who was now her lover.

For a heartbeat, surely no more than that, Jennie gave in to the luxury of letting herself think of him that way. As her lover…

Pain knifed behind her eye, a brutal reminder of the truth and of where that truth would inevitably take her.

She clamped her lips together, biting back the cry that rose in her throat, but there was no stopping the pain. It was red-hot; it was ice-cold. It was worse than it had ever been.

She knew what would happen next. The chills. The shaking. The bits of her vision going gray.

She couldn't let that happen, not while Travis was here.

She bit her lips hard, anything to keep the agony at bay, to let her get away without waking him. She moved quickly, carefully, slipped out from under the shelter of his arm and leg.

He stirred again, mumbled something. She held her breath until he was quiet. Then she rose to her feet, stumbling a little, recovering fast, gritting her teeth against the agonizing throbbing inside her skull.

She wanted to find her robe but there was no time to look for it with the room buried in the blackness of night. The last month, she'd slept with a night-light, a foolish talisman against the dark that was coming for her, but it gave her comfort. She slept with the one-eared toy dog, too; for foolishly sentimental reasons, she'd kept it all through her teen years. It had ended up being the one remnant of a time she'd been whole and well.

Tonight, of course, there was no light. And no toy dog.

Travis had been her talisman. Her comfort.

Carefully, she made her way to the bathroom. She eased the door shut behind her, felt for the shelf over the sink, danced her fingers along it, searching for the little bottle of tablets.

She didn't touch the light switch.

She knew, from experience, that it would hurt her eyes. Besides, it would seep under the door and wake—

Her hand swept over the collection of tiny vials and containers.

"No," she whispered, but it was too late. All of them fell, tumbling into the sink, the sound as loud and clear as if she'd come in here to play the cymbals.

The door flew open. The switch on the wall beside her clicked on; bright light flooded the bathroom.

She flung her arm over her eyes.

"Jennie," Travis said sharply, his voice rough with sleep. "Baby, are you all right?"

"Yes. Yes, I'm fine."

Travis stared at her.

Fine?

He'd been thrown from horses just learning the feel of a man's weight; he'd been ejected from a plane about to go down under enemy fire. He'd been hauled through a public square by a squad of goons determined to make an example of the Yankee pilot who represented everything they despised.

He understood what "fine" meant when it was spoken through tight lips from a face white with pain.

"The hell you are," he growled.

Gently, he clasped her shoulders, then sat her on the closed toilet seat. There was a mess of pill bottles in the sink, plastic, probably, but he checked her face, her hands, her body for blood.

Satisfied that she wasn't hurt, he clasped her wrist to draw her arm from her eyes...

"Don't!"

Her voice was high and sharp.

His heartbeat tripped into double-time. So much for her not being hurt.

"What is it?"

"Nothing. I told you, I'm—"

Travis cursed, gently drew her arm down.

Her eyes were tightly closed.

Okay.

No blood. No cuts. No bruises. But she was paper-white, and shaking, and when he asked her to open her eyes so he could check them, she hissed out a long, low "noooo."

"Jen," he said, squatting down before her, "you have to talk to me. What happened? I woke up, you were gone and then I heard a crash—"

"I—I had a headache." Her voice seemed weak; it sent a chill down his spine. "So I came in here to get—to get something for it."

"Why didn't you put on the light? Why won't you let me see your eyes?"

"I didn't think I'd need the light. I mean, I know where everything is. And my eyes…"

A soft moan broke from her throat.

Travis cursed himself for being an ass.

She was hurting; she'd probably scared herself half to death and instead of helping her, he was asking her a bunch of dumb questions.

"Okay, baby. I get it. You have another headache, like the one you had earlier. And the light…"

The light.

Of course.

A former P.A. had suffered from migraines; she'd told him about the unbearable pain, the way exposure to light made the pain worse.

It was clear that Jennie had the same problem, and that she was having a bad attack.

He rose, switched off the light. He'd turned on the bedside lamp; its soft glow, coming through the open door, was enough for him to see by.

"Don't move," he said in a voice that commanded as much as it comforted.

Quickly, he scooped everything out of the sink—the vials and containers had all stayed closed—carried the stuff into the bedroom and dumped it on the dresser.

There were lots of labels; none of them bore names that were familiar.

"Which of these pills were you looking for?" he said.

Jennie told him.

He found the correct vial, shook a tablet into his hand and went back to her.

"One second, baby."

There was a white plastic cup on the sink. He filled it with water and squatted before her again.

"Open," he said as he brought the pill to her lips.

"I can—"

"Did I ever tell you I was a Boy Scout in my misguided youth?"

Her lips curved in a semblance of a smile.

"Come on. Take the pill. Good girl. Now a drink of water…"

He returned the cup to the sink. Took a neatly-folded face cloth from the towel bar and ran it under cold water from the tap, wrung it out and went back to her.

Her eyes were still closed, her face still pale. He took her hand, turned it up and placed the cool, damp cloth in her palm.

"Lay that over your eyes, honey."

"Travis. You don't have to—"

"'On my honor,'" he said solemnly, "'as a Scout…' You want me to go back on those words?"

She gave a soft, tentative laugh. His heart leaped with joy.

"You? A Boy Scout?"

"Well, no. My brothers and I had our own thing going." *Talk,* he told himself, as he saw color begin coming back into her face, *talk and keep talking, let her hang on to the sound of your voice and maybe it'll help drive away the pain.* "Besides, Mr. Rottweiler, the troop leader, hated us."

"His name was not Mr. Rottweiler!"

Good. Excellent. She was listening to him, concentrating on his stupid jokes. The pill, the compress, were working.

"How come you're so smart, Blondie? His name was Botwilder. Close enough, we figured."

"And he hated you?"

"Yeah, well, see, we'd tipped over his outhouse…"

The breath hissed between her teeth. Travis felt his gut knot; he reached for her, lifted her carefully into his arms. She wound her arms around his neck, buried her face against his throat.

"Nobody has outhouses anymore," she said drowsily.

"Ah, but the Rottweiler did," Travis said briskly as he carried her into the bedroom. "He made his wife and his nineteen kids use it."

Another soft, sweet laugh. Another wish to pump his fist in the air.

"Not nineteen," she said, and yawned.

"Okay. Not nineteen. Eighteen."

He switched off the table lamp. Dawn was breaking—the light in the room was a pale gray.

Gently he lay her down on the narrow bed.

His heart turned over.

She was naked and beautiful, but what he saw, as he drew the duvet over her, was her amazing combination of strength and vulnerability.

"Travis," she whispered.

"I'm here, Jen."

"Thank…"

And then, she was asleep.

He watched her for a minute. Then he whispered, "Okay," reached for his clothes…

Except, he wasn't going anywhere.

He wasn't leaving her.

She needed him.

An image shot into his head.

He, as a very little boy. Sick as hell with something kids get, a virus, a cold, whatever. Waking in the middle of the night, wanting the comfort of a pair of loving arms to hold him, then realizing there were no loving arms, not anymore.

His mom had died, and his father was away saving the world.

Travis dropped the clothes. Pulled back the duvet, climbed into the narrow bed.

Would taking Jennie in his embrace wake her?

He didn't have to decide.

She sighed in her sleep, rolled toward him, burrowed into him as if they had always slept together like this.

He wrapped her in his arms.

Kissed her forehead.

And fell into a deep, dreamless sleep.

CHAPTER EIGHT

SUNLIGHT BLAZED AGAINST Travis's eyelids.

He groaned, rolled onto his belly...

And almost fell off the bed.

His eyes flew open; his brain took survey. Narrow room. Narrow bed. Narrow window. What the hell...?

Then, he remembered.

Jennie. Bringing her home. Making love to her, how incredible it had been.

And hours later, she'd been so ill. That migraine...

"Jennie," he said, as he shot to his feet.

He'd stayed the night to take care of her. Some job he'd done! He hadn't heard her leave the bed. Leave him. Where was she? Was she hurting?

He started for the door.

Dammit, he was naked.

"Clothes," he muttered, looking around the room for the stuff he'd discarded like a wild man last night.

There. On the dresser. A neatly folded stack of all his things.

He grabbed only his khakis, pulled them on, zipped them but didn't bother with the top button, went in search of her...

And found her in the minuscule kitchen, standing with her back to him. Her hair was loose; she had on some kind of oversize T-shirt. Her long legs were bare, as were her feet.

She looked bed-rumpled. Sex-rumpled. And he wanted, more than anything, to sweep her into his arms, take her back to bed.

That he wanted her so with such intensity, even after all the times he'd had her last night, made his words sound gruff.

"Dammit," he growled, "where'd you go?"

She spun toward him. She had a mug in her hand; a dark liquid—coffee, by the welcome smell that permeated the room—sloshed over the rim.

"Travis! You startled—"

He crossed the floor in three quick steps and pulled her into his arms. The coffee sloshed again, this time onto his toes. The stuff was hot, but he didn't care.

"I thought something had happened to you."

"No. I'm fine. I just thought coffee would be a good—"

He kissed her.

She tasted of coffee, cream and sugar.

There'd been times he'd started mornings in Paris with Champagne, in Seville with hot chocolate. But he'd never begun the day with a sweeter flavor on his tongue than the taste of Jennie's mouth.

When he finally lifted his head, her eyes were bright, her lips softly swollen.

"I missed you," he said, before he could think. "Waking up alone wasn't what I had in mind."

She smiled. And blushed.

He loved that blush. It was sexy and innocent at the same time, and made him wonder if he was the first man who'd spent the night with her in his arms.

Just because he was the first man who'd made love to her didn't mean she hadn't done other things with other men.

Hell. Where was he going with that line of thought? He kept reminding himself that he wasn't old-fashioned about women and sex…

Except, it seemed as if he was. About this woman, anyway, and about having sex with her.

About making love with her.

About staying the night in her bed and, come to think of it, how often had he done something like that? Truth was, he could probably count the number of times on the fingers of one hand.

Women tended to get the wrong idea when you spent the night. They read more into it than it deserved.

The way to keep expectations reasonable was to avoid certain trip wires.

Spending the entire night in your lover's bed was one sure trip wire—and why was he thinking of Jennie as his lover? He'd spent two nights with her. That hardly made them "lovers."

Suddenly, the kitchen seemed even smaller than it actually was.

He let go of her, cleared his throat and moved past her to a shelf above the stove where coffee mugs hung from little hooks.

"Great idea," he said briskly. "Making coffee, I mean."

He could feel her looking at him as he filled the mug and added a dollop of cream.

"Yes," she said, after a couple of seconds. "I'm no good at all until I get my morning dose of caffeine."

"Mmm. Same here." There was a teaspoon on the counter. He picked it up, stirred his coffee—but how long could a man take to stir coffee? "So," he said, even more briskly, "you're an early riser, huh?"

"You don't have to do this."

Her voice was low. Something in it made him wince.

"Hey," he said, "why would I turn down a cup of—"

"You don't have to stay. Really. It isn't necessary. I mean, what you did last night—taking care of me, tending to me— that was—it was much, much more than—"

"You were sick."

"Yes. But that doesn't mean—"

He put down the mug and turned toward her. Forget bed-rumpled. Forget sexy. She looked small and fragile and all at once, he hated himself for being such a selfish, unfeeling bastard.

"Come here," he said gruffly, although he was already moving toward her, his arms open.

She went straight into his embrace.

"I'm sorry," she said unsteadily. "I'm not very good at this. I guess I'm not good at it at all. I don't know what I'm supposed to say after—after—"

Travis put his hand under her chin and raised her face to his.

"How about, 'Good morning, Travis. Are you as glad to see me as I am to see you?'"

Her eyes searched his, and then she gave a tremulous smile.

"Are you? Glad to see me? Because—because really, if you just want to leave—"

He silenced her with a kiss.

"Confession time," he said softly. "I'm not sure of what to say, either. I don't—I don't usually..." He cleared his throat. "Spending the entire night in a bed that isn't my own isn't something I've done very often."

He watched her trying to make sense of what he'd said, saw her eyes widen when she did.

"Oh," she said.

And blushed.

God Almighty, that blush!

"Well," she said quickly, "you were—you were kind to do it. I mean, to stay because I—"

"I stayed because I hated the thought of leaving you."

Her lips curved in a smile. What could he possibly do except kiss that smile? And kiss it again, when she sighed, put her hands on his chest and rose toward him.

He wanted to undress her.

Touch her.

Kiss her everywhere.

But she'd been so sick last night…She needed coffee. Food. Not sex.

Except, he didn't want sex.

He wanted to make love to her…

Travis clasped her shoulders, ended the kiss, flashed a quick smile.

"Okay," he said, yes, briskly, and if there was a word that went beyond "briskly," he needed it now. "Time for breakfast."

Her lashes rose. There was a blurred, dreamy look in her eyes.

"To hell with breakfast," he growled, and he drew her against him and kissed her again and again, each kiss deeper, more demanding than the last until she was clinging to him for support, leaning into him, her hands twisted in his hair. "I want you," he said against her mouth.

"That's good," she whispered. "Because I want you, too."

His body, already hard, felt as if it might be turning to stone.

"Your headache…"

She gave a sexy little laugh.

"What headache?" she said, and he swung her into his arms and took her back to bed.

A couple of hours later, they were in his car, on their way to breakfast.

Well, to brunch.

When she'd said she couldn't go with him, that she had to go get her car, he'd phoned the mechanic who worked with him on his 'Vette when it needed something, and asked him to stop by for her car keys.

She'd stayed in the bedroom when the guy showed up but she'd heard Travis describe her old, if honorable, vehicle.

"A tan two-door?" she'd heard the guy say with disbelief, and Travis had said, in solemn tones, that spending half an hour driving it would be good for the guy's soul.

He'd come back to her, still chuckling.

Just remembering it made her smile.

Now she glanced at him from under the curve of her lashes.

They'd completely missed the hours when most people had breakfast.

Instead, they'd spent the time in each other's arms.

And it had been wonderful.

At one point, when she'd sobbed his name and begged him to end the beautiful torment, he'd clasped her wrists, drawn her arms over her head, said—in a sexy growl that had only added to her excitement—that he was never going to end it, that he was going to keep her where she was, on the edge of that high, high precipice…

Even thinking about it made her a little breathless.

Was sex like this for everyone?

She knew it wasn't.

The books said sex was different for all couples but she'd have known that anyway, because sex with Travis was—it was—

Really, there weren't words to describe it.

She'd gone looking for sex.

For the experience of it, because—because time was closing down around her and she couldn't let that happen without knowing what life had not yet shown her, because sex was supposed to be such a powerful part of your existence.

But she had not expected this.

The passion? The excitement? The clinical physiology of orgasm?

Yes, yes, and yes.

But the reality was…

Beyond description. Especially the wonder of those last

few minutes when you felt—you felt as if you were drowning in sensation.

And the rest.

The way you reacted to the sound of your lover's voice. His strength. His tenderness. The feel of his body under your hand, its taste on your mouth.

There was more. Much more, and some of it didn't have a thing to do with sex. Like Travis's smile, or his easy laughter.

Even the way he took control of things.

Of her.

She'd always thought that kind of behavior was male arrogance and, yes, her lover had an arrogance to him, but it wasn't born out of pride or ego or aggression, it was born of the innate ability to lead.

Jennie glanced at him again.

Added to all that, he was beautiful.

She loved watching him.

He did everything with self-assurance. He even drove that way, as he was right now, his attention on the road, his hand light on the steering wheel, the other on the gearshift...

On her hand, lying just beneath his.

What if she hadn't stopped at that awful bar a week ago? What if Travis hadn't been there? What if she hadn't gone along with the game he'd initiated?

What if she'd let fearless Genevieve morph back into cautious Jennie, the Jennie who had not understood how quickly life could change?

Most of all...

Most of all, what if the years still stretched ahead of her, bright and golden in their clarity? What if she was like everyone else, able to reach out and take what she wanted without having to stop and remind herself that she had no right to do so?

Anger flared within her.

And she couldn't afford that anger.

It was too devastating. Too crippling. It stole what little remained of moments and hours and days that might still be filled with happiness.

She'd learned that the hard way.

One minute, you were looking into a future of clear skies and bright promise…and the next, clouds had covered the sun and the future was looking at you, sneering, saying, *Okay, lady, here I am, this is the way it's really gonna be, and what are you gonna to do about it?*

Crumple, had been her first reaction.

But then her alter-ego, for lack of a better term—and what better term would someone who'd taken that double major in psychology and sociology come up with—her alter-ego had said, *Dammit, stand up and fight!*

It didn't change the end game, but it changed the way you got there, head bowed or head high…

"Hey."

They'd pulled to the curb outside a restaurant. Travis was watching her, his dark eyes narrowed.

"Hey yourself," she said, with what she hoped was a smile.

"Are you all right?"

"I'm fine!" she said brightly. Too brightly, perhaps, going by the intensity of his gaze.

"Tell me the truth, honey. Is that migraine back?"

"No. I'm good. Really."

He looked at her for a long minute. Then he flashed that sexy smile, the one that seemed to melt her bones.

"Except when you're bad," he said huskily, "and you're perfect, either way."

She blushed.

He grinned.

"I love the way you do that."

"Do what?"

"The way you blush." He undid his seat belt, leaned in,

undid hers and took her lips in a soft, sweet kiss. "It's one hell of a turn-on."

She blushed even harder. This time, his smile was wicked.

"Keep that up, we're not going to get into the restaurant."

He was right. They wouldn't. If he smiled that way again, kissed her again…

"Jennie," he said in a low voice, because what she was thinking was probably right in her eyes.

What she was feeling was probably only a heartbeat behind, and she couldn't let him see that because it was impossibly out of the question, it was not what he'd signed on for and, oh God, it was far, far more than she'd ever even considered…

"You going to feed me, Wilde?" she said, reaching for the door handle, laughing in a way that she hoped didn't sound as phony to him as it did to her. "Or let me swoon away from hunger right here, in your car, with everybody in Dallas walking by?"

"The only swooning I want you doing is the kind that happens when I take you in my arms," he said.

But he wasn't laughing.

Neither was she.

They stared at each other for what seemed an eternity.

Then Travis cleared his throat, stepped out of the car and the world began spinning again.

She ordered yogurt and fresh fruit.

He ordered pancakes, bacon and eggs.

"The menu says they use only certified humane, free-range eggs," she said, after the waitress had brought them orange juice.

Travis raised an eyebrow.

"And that's good, right?"

She nodded. "Absolutely. Did you ever see any of the documentaries about how chickens are raised?"

"No," he said quickly. From the look on her face, he was happy that he hadn't.

"Back home—"

"Where's that?"

"New Hampshire."

"Ah. Thought I heard a touch of New England in that accent of yours."

She wrinkled her nose.

"You're the one with the accent, cowboy, not me."

He grinned. "Anyway, back home…?"

"I spent part of a summer working at an egg farm." Her smile faded; a little shudder went through her. "'Farm' turned out to be the wrong way to describe it. It was an eye opener."

He'd never thought about it before. Now he did.

"Yes," he said, "I'll bet."

Their meal arrived, her bowl of yogurt heaped with big, shiny strawberries. He watched as she plucked one from the heap, brought it to her lips and bit into it.

Crimson juice ran down her chin. She got to it, fast, with her napkin.

He thought about how he could have got to it faster, with his tongue.

Not a good thing to think about, in a public place.

"So," he said quickly shifting a little in the leather booth, "is that why you're such an early riser?" She looked at him blankly and why wouldn't she? Talk about non sequiturs… but it was the best he could do on the spur of the moment. "You were up with the sun this morning."

"Oh." She smiled. "It has nothing to do with chickens. It's academia." Her smile became a chuckle at the look on his face. "I have three early classes a week. I'm a T.A. A teaching—"

"A teaching assistant."

"Uh-huh. It's a grad course. The Psychology of Male-Female Relationship Patterns."

Travis nodded. Male-female relationships. He could almost feel his appetite fading.

"Must be—"

"Deadly dull."

His eyebrows rose. She laughed.

"I know I shouldn't say that but it is." She brought the teaspoon to her mouth. "And what do you…" Her face pinkened.

"What?" he said, his eyes on the spoon, imagining what the coolness of the yogurt would be like in the warmth of her mouth.

"I only just realized…I don't know anything about you."

"You know everything about me," he said in a low voice. "Everything that matters."

"No. Seriously. If you and I—"

"Honey." His gaze went from the spoonful of creamy yogurt to her rosy lips. "Save me here, will you? Put that yogurt in your mouth so I can stop working up a sweat thinking about it."

"Thinking…?"

Man, what a mistake to have told her that. She was blushing again. He'd made love to her enough to know her chest and breasts turned that same rose-petal pink when she had an orgasm, when his lovemaking caused her orgasm…

"Do it fast," he said hoarsely.

She put the spoon down.

"Travis. Don't look at me like that."

"Like what?"

"Like—like—" She caught her bottom lip between her teeth. "Tell me—tell me about yourself."

He grinned. "Change in conversation, huh?"

"Absolutely. Come on. Tell me about Travis Wilde."

"There's not much to tell."

Jennie rolled her eyes. "You don't really think I'll fall for that, 'shucks, ma'am, ah'm jest a plain cowboy' stuff, do you?"

He burst out laughing.

"Talk about accents…Is that how guys in Texas sound?"

"Some of them." She smiled. "But not you. Were you born here?"

"You mean, am I an honest-to-God Texan?" He put his knife and fork across his plate, pushed it aside, reached for his coffee. "I am. I was born here. Well, not here. Not in Dallas. I was born in Wilde's Crossing?"

"A town with your name?"

"Wildes have been in Texas a long time, honey. You listen to my old man tell the story, we've been here ever since Thor the Hammer wrecked his longship on the Corpus Christi bar."

Jennie grinned. "No, he didn't."

He grinned back. "Okay. Maybe not, but yeah, we go back a bit."

"Are you ranchers?"

Amazing, he thought. He knew every inch of this woman's luscious body, she knew his, and yet, they were only just having this conversation.

"We have a place in Wilde's Crossing. *El Sueño*."

"The Dream."

Somehow or other, that she knew what the words meant pleased him.

"Yes. Do you know Spanish?"

"I had two years of it in high school."

"Ah."

"Plus two years of German. My father said, if I was going into science, it was a good idea to know German."

Travis cocked his head. "'The Psychology of Male-Female Relationship Patterns' is science?"

"Yes. No. I mean, there's this whole controversy, whether psych and sociology are sciences or not…" She made a face. "Travis Wilde. You're trying to change the subject."

He sat back, sighed, drank some coffee.

"Okay. I was born in Wilde's Crossing. I grew up on *El*

Sueño. I liked ranching well enough but math always fascinated me…"

He paused. Math? How come he was telling her that? Women had made it clear that "math" wasn't sexy. Being a finance guy, an investor, was.

"Math," she said. "If only I'd known you in high school." She smiled. "I'd have flunked calculus if it hadn't been for Mary Jane Baxter."

Travis tried not to smile. She was full of information, his Jennie; all you had to do was find the right button and out it came.

"Mary Jane Baxter?"

"A girl I knew. See, we did a trade. I coached her in English Lit. She coached me in Calc."

"Sounds like a good deal all around."

"It was." She sat back in the booth. "But you're not a math teacher. Not with that car and condo."

"No. Well, for a while I was in the Air Force."

"Really?"

He nodded. "I flew planes. Jets." Her eyes widened. "Fighter jets," he added, watching her face.

Hell, he was boasting. He knew the effect that bit of news had on women; if their eyes glazed over at the thought of a guy doing math, they positively glowed on hearing a guy was a jet jockey—and wasn't that pathetic? That he wanted to impress her?

"Did you serve in the war?"

He nodded, all his boasting forgotten.

"Yeah."

"That must have been hard. Seeing things. Doing things…"

Her voice was low. Her eyes said she understood that flying a fighter jet in battle left a man with memories that weren't entirely pleasant.

"Yeah. Sometimes, it was."

"But other times, it must have been wonderful."

He smiled. It occurred to him that it was a long time since he'd thought about that part of it.

"What's it like? To soar over the world?"

"Well," he said…

And he told her.

About the sense of freedom. The joy. About the sight of the earth, far below. About the first time he'd taken the controls from his instructor.

"It wasn't a fighter jet, it was a crop duster. See, I loved planes, even when I was a kid. And this guy used to work for us—"

"For *El Sueño*."

She'd remembered the name of the place he still thought of as home. For some reason, that pleased him.

"Exactly. He taught me to fly, and then I worked like crazy all one summer on another ranch, earning enough money so I could pay for real lessons…" He paused. "I'm talking too much."

"No. Oh, no! I love hearing about you as a little boy. I can almost picture you, boots, jeans, a cowboy hat—"

Travis laughed.

"Bumps, bruises and dirt. That was me. My brothers, too. Our mom used to say we were the reason Johnson & Johnson made Band-Aids…"

His words trailed away.

He'd told Jennie more about himself in ten minutes than he'd ever told anyone in a lifetime.

"It must be nice to have brothers."

He cleared his throat.

"Don't let them hear me admit it," he said with the kind of grin that made it clear he was joking, "but they're great guys."

"Did they go into the Air Force, too?"

"Caleb went into some government agency he can only tell you about if he kills you after." She laughed; he took her hand and brought it to his lips. "Jake went into the Army. He flew combat helicopters." His smile tilted. "He was wounded. Badly. And, for a while, he lost his way…" He paused. "I—I guess I kind of lost mine, too."

His own admission stunned him.

He had never said anything like that, not even to Jake or Caleb…but it was true.

He'd always been into risk: high stakes poker had given him the money to start his investment business, but the risks that came of being part of a war nobody could quite get their heads around had affected him.

Coming home and putting everything on the line—all his considerable winnings, his reputation, his mathematical ability—had been, in some dark, crazed way, a means of taking control of his life.

Risk everything, win everything.

All you had to be sure of was whether or not the risk was worth taking…

"Travis?"

Jennie's voice was soft.

All at once, he felt as if every risk he'd ever taken had been nothing compared to this…

"Yes." He cleared his throat, searched blindly for a way to change the subject. "Tell me about you."

"There's not a lot to tell," she said, lying so easily it terrified her. "As I said, I'm from New Hampshire. No brothers, no sisters. Not like you, with all those brothers—"

"Only two. And three sisters. Emily, Lissa and Jaimie. Well, half sisters, but we never think of them like that. Our mother died and our father married again. We lost her, too."

"It's hard, losing your parents." Jennie paused. "Mine died in a car crash when I was eighteen."

Travis wrapped both her hands in his.

"Leaving you alone?"

"Yes." She cleared her throat. "Tell me about your father."

There was more to her story; he was certain of it, but if she needed to change the subject, he'd let her.

"Ah." Travis waggled his eyebrows. "The old man is a four-star general."

"Oh, boy."

"Oh, boy, indeed. You can't imagine what it's like, growing up under the eye of somebody who thinks he's perfect."

Jennie smiled. "Actually, I can. Well, not exactly. My folks never said they were perfect—but they were. A pair of professors. Dad was a classicist. Mom was a medievalist. Brilliant, both of them. They had me late in life, so they were kind of overprotective." She sighed. "And when I said I wanted to go into psych and sociology—"

"I bet that went over about as well as when I said I was leaving the military to start my own investment firm."

"Exactly. I might as well have said I wanted to, I don't know, to play in a sandbox for the rest of my life."

"But you're happy, doing—" he grinned "—doing whatever it is you do."

Jennie laughed.

"I teach. Well, I will teach…"

Her smile, so lovely and wide, faded. Darkness filled her eyes.

"Honey? What is it?"

"Nothing," she said. "Nothing at all."

"Is it your headache? Is it back?"

"No." She blinked, smiled, but he could see tears glittering in her eyes. "I'm fine. Really. I'm absolutely fine."

He moved fast, leaned over the table, all but pulled her into his arms.

"Yes," he said gruffly, "you are," and when her tears began spilling down her cheeks, he took out his wallet, tossed a stack of bills on the table and did the only thing a man standing on the edge of a precipice could do.

He took her out of the restaurant, took her home to his place where he held her in his arms and made love to her until the tears she wept were tears of joy.

CHAPTER NINE

HE WANTED HER to spend the night with him.

She said that she couldn't.

"I have to go home," she said as she lay in his arms in a lounger on the terrace.

"It's almost midnight. That means it's almost Sunday, and Sunday's a day when nobody has to do anything."

She laughed. "You make that sound so logical."

"It *is* logical. Would a mathematician say anything that wasn't?"

"You're an investment banker, Travis Wilde. You play the stock market. What's logical about that?"

Travis clapped his hand to his heart.

"You wound me, madam."

Jennie laughed. "Seriously. I have to go home."

"Why?" he said, trying to make light of it because she had no way of knowing he hardly ever asked a woman to spend the night in his bed—and he was still amazed that having her do that was what he wanted. He kissed the tip of her nose. "Have to feed the cat?"

"I wish," she said, a little wistfully.

"You like cats, huh?"

"I like animals. But—"

"But?"

"But, I never had one. My mother said pets would make

a mess. And when I went away to college, you couldn't have pets in the dorm."

Travis thought of the big mutt he'd found wandering on campus his freshman year, and brought back to his dorm suite.

"Dogs are not allowed," the R.A. had said with authority.

"Right," Travis had replied…and moved the dog into his room for the rest of the semester, when he'd taken him home to *El Sueño*.

But Jennie wouldn't have done that.

She was a good girl, and good girls didn't break rules…

Except for the one about walking into a bar to pick up a guy and hand over your virginity.

Why? Why had she done something so out of character? Because now that he knew her, he could not imagine she would ever have done such a thing.

There had to be a reason.

She was keeping part of herself a secret. He knew it. And it worried him.

"Travis," she said softly, lifting her head from his shoulder and smiling at him. "You look so serious. What are you thinking?"

He smiled back at her.

"I'm trying to come up with some brilliantly creative reason that will convince you to stay."

She wanted to. Desperately. Hours had gone by since the headache and it might not return for even more hours. Still, if it did…

You need to keep your meds with you, Jennifer, the doctor had said, but carrying around a container of tablets and capsules would be a constant reminder of—of what was happening to her, and she wasn't ready for that.

Not yet

He brushed his lips lightly over hers.

"Now who's looking serious?"

Jennie forced a smile.

"I'm thinking."

"A dangerous habit—unless you're thinking of changing your mind about leaving me."

A swell of emotion rose inside her.

She didn't want to leave him. Not ever. How could you leave a man like this?

He kissed her, slid his hand under the shirt he'd given her to wear. She caught her breath as he stroked her nipples.

"Travis—"

"I'm just helping you come up with a reason to stay."

She laughed.

"You're a bad influence on me," she said, but it wasn't true. He was a wonderful influence. In all her life, she had never been this happy, felt so alive...

Tears welled swiftly, dangerously in her eyes. She tried to bury her face against him before he could see them but she wasn't quick enough.

"Sweetheart. What is it?"

"Allergies," she said brightly. "Nothing to worry about."

And, really, there was nothing to worry about, because what was the point? She couldn't change fate, couldn't change life...

Couldn't change what was happening in her heart, each time Travis kissed her or touched her or said her name.

"Stay with me," he said.

Do what your heart tells you, her alter-ego whispered.

And what it told her was to stay.

In the morning, when he staggered into the john, eyes half closed because it was Sunday and surely there was a law against fully waking up early on Sundays, Travis finished what he'd gone into the bathroom to do, flushed the toilet, washed his hands, reached for a face towel and came up, instead, with something small and silken.

His eyes flew open.

It was a pair of white panties.

Jennie's.

Evidently, she'd rinsed them last night and left them to dry.

Travis looked at them. So honest. So unsophisticated.

So Jennie.

A funny feeling swept over him.

Among the few women who'd ever spent the night, a couple had left things on the vanity. A compact. A lipstick. He wasn't an overly fastidious man but seeing those things in what was his space had irritated him no end.

Seeing Jennie's panties on his towel rack sent a warmth through his veins.

He liked seeing them there.

He liked seeing her in his bed.

And he was old enough, wise enough, to know that liking those things could be dangerous to a man's stability and sanity.

Okay. Time for her to leave. She'd stayed the night. They'd made love when they'd first gone to bed, then during the night.

He'd give her a cup of coffee, then drive her home. Phone her in a few days, ask her to dinner, to a movie, whatever.

It was a good plan, but it fell apart as soon as he went back into the bedroom and saw her.

She'd just come awake; her eyes were sleepy-looking, her hair was mussed, and when she saw him, she smiled.

"Good morning," she said softly.

Travis shook his head as he made his way to her.

"It isn't," he said solemnly, "because we haven't yet performed a vital morning ritual."

Her eyebrows rose. "What ritual?"

"This one," he said, and he took her in his arms and kissed her, and she returned his kiss with such tenderness that he could have sworn he felt his heart swell.

* * *

They spent the morning reading the papers, eating omelets Jennie made after she'd opened the fridge, rolled her eyes and finally unearthed half a dozen eggs, what remained of a pint of cream, four English muffins, a stick of butter and the biggest find of all, a chunk of still-usable Gruyère to add to the eggs.

There was other stuff, too: a bunch of little white cardboard containers Travis thought might have contained left-over take-out Tex-Mex.

"Unless it's take-out Chinese," he said apologetically.

"Hard to tell, I guess."

"Yuck," she said, dumping the containers in the trash.

"Hey," Travis said, his hand on his heart, "what can I tell you? Cooking isn't my thing."

Thankfully, it seemed that coffee was.

He had two pounds of Kona beans in the freezer, a grinder in the cupboard and a pot with more dials and buttons on it than Jennie had ever seen in her life.

She rolled her eyes again but admitted he got points for not completely destroying her faith in starting the day right.

Travis grinned, came up behind her, wrapped his arms around her and lightly bit the nape of her neck.

"I thought what we did a little while ago definitely started the day right."

"Behave yourself," she said sternly, but she leaned back against him and tilted her head up for a kiss.

After breakfast, they showered again. His shower was big enough for a dozen people, she said, and he gave a mock growl, took her in his arms and said he'd fight off anybody foolish enough to try to share the shower with them because she belonged strictly to him.

He meant the words as a joke.

But once he'd said them, he stopped smiling. Jennie did, too.

"Strictly to me," he said gruffly, and he made love to her against the glass wall, beneath the kiss of the warm spray.

He wanted to take her out.

Well, what he really wanted was to take her to bed, again, but he knew how much he'd love walking down a street with her beside him.

He thought about the things the women in his past had liked to do.

Did she want to go window-shopping? She wrinkled her nose. Stroll through a flea market? Another wrinkle of that cute little nose. How about a walk in the park? A drive?

She chewed on her lip.

"What?" he asked.

She hesitated. "I don't suppose...I mean, I heard a couple of other T.A.'s talking...No. Never mind. It's silly. A drive would be—"

"Nothing's silly, if it'll make you happy." Travis took her hand and brought it to his lips. What did she want to do? Go to see some chick flick, probably. Well, fine. Not fun but he could surely survive—

"Six Flags," she blurted.

For a second or two, he was lost.

"Six flags of what?" He blinked. "You mean, the amusement park?"

She nodded. Her eyes were round and bright.

"Could we?"

Travis grinned, put his arm around her shoulders and gave her a loud, smacking kiss.

"A woman after my own heart!"

"Oh, my," Jennie kept saying, as they strolled through the park, hand in hand.

Everything made her squeal with delight. The grilled turkey legs. The funnel cakes. The giant hot dogs.

And the rides.

They drew her like a candy store drew kids.

"Can we watch?" she kept saying, and Travis would say sure, of course, and while she watched the rides and the riders, he watched her.

Was it possible this was all new for her?

"Honey?" he said as she stood, head tilted back, mouth forming a perfect "O," her fingernails digging into his hand as terrified people shrieked and screamed with delight while plummeting earthward on a parachute ride, "haven't you ever been to a place like this before?"

She shook her head, but her eyes stayed locked to the parachute tower.

"No."

"Little parks only? Okay. Maybe there isn't anything like this in New—"

"My parents didn't approve of amusement parks."

Her parents. The duo that had been upset because she hadn't wanted to be a doctor or a lawyer or an accountant.

"Well, how about local fairs? You know, Ferris wheels. Old-fashioned roller coasters."

Jennie shook her head.

"Not those, either. My parents were very protective, remember?"

"Aha," he said, trying to imagine how it must have been for her to grow up in such a closed-off world.

"They meant well," she said quickly, because his "aha" had dripped with meaning. "But they always, you know, careful I didn't do anything that might be, you know, dangerous or, you know, risky, or—"

"What I know," Travis said gently, drawing her into the curve of his arm, "is that they wanted to protect you."

She nodded. "Exactly. But—but—"

"But," he said, smiling, trying to make light of what she'd missed, "life is short."

She looked up at him, her eyes suddenly dark with something he couldn't read.

"Yes. It is. And when I—when I realized that, I knew there were so many things I'd never done, that I wanted to know about…"

Like making love.

She didn't say it.

He did.

And when he did, she nodded.

"I wanted to know about sex," she said in a low voice. "But what I learned about was—was making love. And it wouldn't have been making love if I hadn't found—" Her words stumbled to a halt. "Oh, God! Travis. I didn't mean that the way it sounded. Please, I swear, I'm not trying to—"

He took her in his arms and kissed her.

It was either that or say something he couldn't imagine saying to a woman he'd met a week ago, something he'd never imagined saying to any woman ever, or at least not for maybe the next hundred years.

Something that made no sense, he told himself, but as she melted against him, he knew that nothing had made sense since the night she'd walked into that bar.

Nothing—except the sweet, sweet joy he felt, holding his Jennie in his arms.

After a while, he figured she was happy just looking at everything.

Logical.

For a girl who'd never so much as ridden a Ferris wheel, going on one of the park's big rides would surely be daunting. That was fine with him. Just being together made the day perfect—and when he saw her staring at somebody munching on one of those enormous turkey legs, he figured he knew a way to make her smile.

"Lunch," he said.

Jennie looked at him.

"You get your choice of gourmet treats, madam. A turkey leg. A hot dog—though you have to understand, they won't do 'em with the sophisticated panache of the Wilde Brothers—"

She laughed.

A good sign, because she'd been very quiet for the last twenty or thirty minutes.

"Or fried chicken. A hamburger. Pretty much any non-PC, artery-cloggin' goody your heart desires—"

"The roller coaster."

"Huh?"

"The wooden one. Where we were a little while ago. The one called Judge Something-Or-Other." Her eyes were shining. "Can we ride it?"

Travis hesitated. "Honey. You sure you want to start with something like that? There are easier rides to—"

Jennie bounced on her toes. The last time he'd seen somebody do that, it had been his sister Lissa, aged three or four, pleading for him to let her ride his horse instead of her pony.

He hadn't been able to say "no" then.

And he sure as hell couldn't say it now.

She loved riding that roller coaster.

She screamed and shrieked, and laughed with such joy that he forgot he'd given up nonsense like amusement parks a long time ago and laughed along with her.

"Again," she said when the ride ended.

They rode the coaster again.

And then they rode everything else, or damn near everything else, before Travis said, "Enough," took her in his arms for probably the hundredth time that day, kissed her and said it was time they took a break, ate something, drank something while he told himself he was being, yes, protective, but not the way her parents had been.

But he understood how they'd felt.

Someone as good and sweet as Jennie deserved to be protected.

"Okay," she said. And laughed. "Actually, I just realized—I'm starving! I could eat a horse!"

"Them's fightin' words, here in Texas," Travis said solemnly.

They ate tacos. Fried chicken. One of those turkey legs.

"It's from a brontosaurus, not a turkey," Jennie said, chomping into it.

Travis watched her eat and tried not to smile.

"More?" he said politely, after she'd finished the leg.

She thought about the giant hot dogs she'd seen, glistening on the grill. Then she remembered something Travis had said.

"What did you mean about the Wilde Brother's hot dogs?"

He laughed.

"When we were kids, Jacob, Caleb and I would cook up these feasts."

"Feasts? With hot dogs?"

"Have some faith, woman. Would we call it a feast if it only involved hot dogs? These were special. We fried 'em." He laughed at the expression on her face. "Actually, I did. Jake made the fried cheese sandwiches. Caleb was the marshmallow expert." Travis brought his thumb and index finger together. "Dee-lish-ee-oh-so!"

Jennie reached for a napkin.

"That did it. I'm full."

He grinned.

"Amazing. You should be popping out of your jeans by now." He held out his hand. "Come on. Let's get some lemonade."

They found a stand, bought huge plastic glasses of lemonade and found a quiet spot on a bench beneath a tree.

"So," Travis said, "what's your professional opinion of amusement parks, Dr. Cooper?"

Her smile, so bright during the past hours, seemed to dim a little.

"I don't have a doctorate yet."

"But you will."

She shrugged her shoulders. "You never know."

"Well, true. Life's unpredictable, but—"

"I had a wonderful time today!"

He smiled, reached for her hand.

"Me, too."

"All those rides…" Her eyes shone. "What do you call them? Thrill rides?"

"Right."

"Well, they're definitely thrilling. But basically, they're safe. I mean, the parks wouldn't have them if they weren't. Right?"

"Right," he said again, and wondered where the conversation was going because, clearly, there was something in the wind.

"What I mean is," she said slowly, "there's no real risk."

Travis grinned. "Got it. Nope. No real risk, so it's safe to tell your folks that— Oh. Honey. I'm sorry. I forgot."

"It's okay," she said softly. "That's the way life is. You're born, you die…"

She fell silent.

Travis thought he felt her hand tremble in his.

"Okay," he said briskly, "we're out of here. You've had enough sun and enough risk for the day."

"No. I mean, that's what I was saying. There really isn't any risk in taking these rides. It's wonderful," she added quickly. "I mean, I had more fun today…" She looked at him. "I never actually did anything risky."

Travis nodded. The conversation was on track again.

"But you have," she said. "Haven't you?"

"Well—"

"Did you ever go bungee jumping?"

"Yes. And it's not all it's cracked up to—"

"Back country skiing. Scuba diving. Rock climbing. Swimming with sharks."

"Jennie." His tone was harsh; he hadn't meant it to be. "Where are you going with this?"

"I want to try something risky."

A muscled knotted in his jaw.

"You already did. You got all dressed up, walked into a bar—"

Her face crumpled. She sprang to her feet.

He caught her by the wrist.

"I said it wrong, dammit. I didn't mean it the way you think." When she shook her head, he rose, too. "What I'm saying is that anything might have happened to you that night, anything at all. And the thought of something happening to you, something or someone hurting you…" Travis clasped her shoulders and turned her toward him. "Do you know how much you mean to me?" he said in a thick voice. "Do you have any idea how important you've become to me?"

She shook her head.

"You don't know me. We've only been together—"

"I know how long we've been together. But I know something else, as well." He looked deep into her eyes. "This— you and me—this isn't—it isn't just a man and a woman and—and sex—"

She shook her head and tried to turn away. He wouldn't let her.

"I'm saying it wrong, dammit. What I mean is—"

"I know what you mean. I—I feel it, too." Tears glittered like stars in her eyes. "I never meant for this to happen," she whispered. "That I'd find someone like you, that I'd find such happiness—"

He kissed her.

Gently. Only their lips met, as if touching her might shatter the moment.

And as he kissed her, he tasted the salt of her tears.

Something ran through him, an emotion so new, so rare that it stunned him, and with it came a question.

Could everything a man thought he wanted out of life completely shift in little more than a week?

Even asking the question was dangerous.

Travis put his arm around Jennie, held her to his side as they headed back to his car.

Dangerous, sure.

But as he'd learned years ago, you could say that about anything that was really worth doing. Or having.

Life was all about risk.

What he hadn't known was that, if a man was really lucky, he might just stumble across one special risk that had the power to change his life, forever.

CHAPTER TEN

ALMOST A MONTH later, on a gray, rainy morning, that was all he could think about.

Risks.

The kind he'd always taken.

Not the kind he was taking now.

He'd been a wild kid, the same as his brothers. But none of them had ever done anything cruel or stupid and—predictably—their streaks of wildness had eventually been channeled into positive stuff.

Jake, flying helicopters and now running *El Sueño* as well as his own ranch.

Caleb, taking the darker route into secret government service and now taking on law cases that drew headlines.

He, Travis, flying jets and then going into big-time finance.

Risky things, all. But still, with an edge of predictability to them.

Not anymore.

This wasn't predictable.

What he felt for Jennie.

What he believed she felt for him.

It made what had existed between him and the girl who'd written him that Dear John letter years ago, laughable.

She had never been a serious part of his life.

They'd come together as much because of his glamorous

status as a fighter pilot as her flashy looks. He'd never really looked ahead and envisioned her as part of his real life.

Jennie was already in his real life.

She wasn't just his lover, she was his friend.

Hell, she was his roommate.

Her toothbrush hung beside his.

They were—it still amazed him—they were living together, and they hadn't been apart for more than a few hours each day for the last three and a half weeks.

So, yes, this was a very different kind of risk.

It involved putting aside an entire way of life, one that was free of restraint or rules or obligations to anyone but himself.

It involved, he thought, staring out his office window on a rainy morning, something he'd never imagined himself doing.

Living with a woman.

It wasn't that he'd never considered it. The thought had certainly crossed his mind before, not often, but there'd been times it had, at the start of a relationship…

And, man, he'd always hated that word—relationship—but that was what this was, a relationship.

He and Jennie were living together.

And he loved it.

Coming home to her each night. Starting the day with her each morning.

He loved it.

Travis rose from his chair, tucked his hands into his trouser pockets and paced slowly around his office.

Talk about a shocker…

Until now, living with a woman had never gone beyond casual speculation.

The simple truth was, the excitement of an affair faded. The fun wore away. The prospect of spending all his time with one woman pretty much 24/7 lost its appeal.

It had never been the fault of any of his lovers.

It was just the way things were.

Man wasn't meant for monogamy. *He* wasn't, at any rate…

He paused at the floor-to-ceiling, wall-of-glass window, and stared out at the gray Dallas skyline.

Turned out, what he'd been meant for was Jennie.

They went to sleep in each other's arms and woke that same way. They ate together. Talked about mundane stuff like where to have dinner, complicated stuff like global warming. They went out, stayed in, listened to music, did all the things couples did and bachelors didn't…

And he loved it.

Especially coming home to her at night, when just see-ing her smile, having her go into his arms, was more than enough to smooth whatever jagged edges the day might have left in its wake.

Jennie was living with him.

She had been, for almost a month.

The excitement? Still there. The fun? Of course. But there was more than that to it.

Being together was…He searched for the word.

It was joy.

The arrangement, for lack of a better word, had come about without plan.

It had started that Sunday when they'd gone to Six Flags.

They'd gone for a drive afterward.

Then they'd stopped for supper at a little Thai place he knew. The place was six tables big, with no pretensions at being anything but a Mom-and-Pop joint where the decor rated a zero but the food was Bangkok-perfect.

It turned out Thai food was new to Jennie.

How you could get through college and grad school with-out having Pad Thai or Tom Yum Goong or was beyond him, but then he remembered those overly-protective parents who'd raised her to be cautious about everything, and he understood.

Sex. Roller coasters. Thai food.

He teased her, asked her if there was anything more he

was going to introduce her to and she looked at him in a way that was suddenly completely serious.

Then, she laughed and said if there were, she'd let him know.

If she were six decades older, he'd have said she was working on a bucket list.

She wasn't, of course.

She was simply a woman learning about life.

He'd ordered for them both. *Tom Kha Gai*. Red Curry. *Pad Thai*.

"Oh, my," she said, after she'd tasted the soup.

"As in, 'Oh, my, this is good'? Or, 'Oh, my, I don't like this at all!'"

"Are you kidding? It's amazing!"

She was what was amazing, he'd thought, watching her.

They ate from each other's plates and talked all through the meal, about Texas and New England, nothing special, and when they left the restaurant, he'd driven her to her apartment.

"I don't want to leave you," he'd said, at her door.

"I don't want that, either," she'd said softly. "Come in, just for a while."

He'd taken a deep breath.

"I have a better idea," he'd said, no planning, no preparation, but as he'd said the words, he'd known they were right. "Pack something for tomorrow. Come home with me."

She'd hesitated, long enough so his heart had almost stopped beating.

"I can't," she'd finally said.

"You can do anything that makes you happy," he'd said softly. "Unless being with me won't make you happy."

Silence.

Then she'd gone up on her toes and kissed him.

She'd packed a summer skirt. A T-shirt. Sandals. Underwear. Makeup, shampoo, what he thought of as girl stuff, though he knew better than actually to call it that.

A man didn't grow up with sisters without learning something.

Finally, she'd put her laptop computer in its case, added a couple of books and a stack of printed notes.

"Ready," she'd said, and again, without planning or analyzing it, he'd heard himself suggest she add a few more things to what she'd packed.

"You know, just in case you, ah, you decided to stay a few days…"

It had been one of those time-stands-still moments, he silent, she staring at him through wide eyes.

Then, with typical Jennie-directness, she'd said, very softly, "Are you asking me to live with you?"

With untypical directness, at least when it came to women, he'd said, "Yes."

She hadn't gone back to her place since that night, except when he'd driven her there so she could pick up more of her things.

He'd tried to take her shopping. At Neiman Marcus, of course, but she wouldn't let him.

She was independent, his Jennie, so he compensated by buying her gifts, then telling her, eyes wide with innocence, that whatever he'd bought was on sale and couldn't be returned.

He'd done it again last night, handed her a gift-wrapped small box at dinner at the Thai place that had become a favorite.

She'd opened the box, gasped at the gold bracelet and heart inside, and looked at him with shining eyes.

"Travis. I can't—"

"You have to," he'd said. "It's that damned no-returns policy."

Her lips had curved in a smile.

"I love it," she'd said. "Thank you."

"You're welcome," he'd said, and without warning, he'd

suddenly imagined her opening an even smaller box, one that held a diamond solitaire.

Their food had arrived at that moment, and they'd spent the rest of the meal talking.

Actually, he'd done most of the talking.

He'd found himself telling her about the ten thousand acres of land for sale in Wilde's Crossing, about how he was considering buying it.

"I love what I do," he'd said, "and I'll always go on doing it, but ranching is in my blood."

"Must be the Viking DNA," she'd said solemnly but with a little smile in her eyes, and he'd laughed and then, without planning to, he'd heard himself ask, very casually, how she felt about open spaces, about horses and dogs and kids, which were pretty much the staples of ranch life...

And realized he was holding his breath as he waited for her answer.

"I grew up watching old John Wayne movies," she'd finally said, in a small voice. "My father owned every one. And—and I used to think how wonderful if must be, to saddle a horse and ride and ride and ride without ever reaching the boundaries of your own land, and then to ride home to a house full of love and laughter, to the arms of a man you adored..."

Her voice had trembled. Her eyes had darkened. He'd reached for her hand.

He'd come within a heartbeat of saying that she could, if she married him, but a crowded restaurant wasn't where a man wanted to tell a woman he loved her.

Besides, the look on her face troubled him.

Something was wrong.

Jennie definitely had a secret, and it was not a good one.

He'd sensed it before, several times, but he'd never pushed her to reveal it because, back then, he'd still believed in separation. In independence. In being responsible for oneself and nobody else.

Not anymore.

She had a secret that made her unhappy and, by God, it was time he knew what it was so he could deal with it.

Had she been in jail? Was she on the run for a crime? Was somebody after her?

Impossible things, all of them, but there was a darkness haunting her, and she had yet to share it with him.

Didn't she realize that whatever it was, he would deal with it?

That he would go on loving her?

Because he did love her. He adored her.

And she loved him, too.

He could see it in her smile. In the way she curled into his arms at night and responded to his kisses in the morning. It was even in the way she said his name.

It was time to say the words.

Tonight, he was going to tell her that he loved her. And after she'd told him she loved him, too, he would ask her what was causing her such anguish.

Her headaches, painful as they were, never brought such sadness to her eyes, but her headaches seemed more frequent.

"Have you taken your medicine?" he'd say, and she'd say yes, she had, and then she'd change the subject.

Except, last night, a muffled sound had awakened him.

The place on the bed beside him was empty.

He'd risen quickly, gone into the bathroom, found her huddled on the closed toilet, trembling, her face white, teeth chattering.

Terror had torn at his gut.

"Sweetheart," he'd said, going down on his knees before her. "What is it?" No answer. He'd reached forward, swept her tangled hair back from her face. "Is it a headache?"

"Yes," she'd whispered.

"Did you take a pill?"

Another yes.

He'd risen to his feet.

"I'm calling my doctor," he'd said, and she'd grabbed his arm and gasped out, "No! I don't need a doctor!"

The hell she didn't.

But he hadn't wanted to upset her, so he'd scooped her into his arms, carried her to bed, brought her a cold pack—he'd started keeping them in the freezer—and held her in his arms until she'd fallen asleep.

Dammit, he thought now, as he sat down behind his desk again.

He'd been so caught up in thinking about how much he loved her, how he was going to tell her so, tonight, that he'd lost sight of what he should have done first thing this morning.

She didn't want to see his doctor? Okay. He couldn't force her to do it, but his physician was an old pal. He and Ben had gone to the same high school, played on the football team. They'd gone to the same university, taken some of the same undergrad courses before Ben went into medical school and Travis set his sights on aerospace engineering..

He'd go see Ben, tell him about Jennie, tell him the name of the meds she was taking and find out if there wasn't something a lot stronger and better.

No way could he go on watching the woman he loved suffer...

The woman he loved.

It felt so good to know that he loved her. To know he was going to tell her he loved her—

His cell phone rang.

He grabbed it, didn't take time to check the screen.

"Honey?"

"Sweetie," his brother Jake purred. "I didn't know you cared."

Travis sat back.

"Jacob. What's up?"

"From hot to cold in less than a minute. Travis, my man, you're breakin' my heart."

Travis laughed.

"Okay. Let's start again. Hey, Jake, great to hear from you. How're things going?"

"Tonight's what's going," Jake said. "I thought the three of us could get together at that place near Caleb's office."

"Yeah. Well, sorry, but—"

"Trav. You were the one accusing us of ditching the Friday night stuff but we got together last week and the week before, and you were the guy who was missing."

True. Very true. Travis rubbed his hand over his forehead.

"The thing is, I, ah, I have something going on…"

"Does it involve 'honey'?"

Jake's tone barely masked his laughter—and his curiosity. Travis took a deep breath. What the hell, he decided, maybe it was time.

"Tell you what. I'll meet you guys there. I won't stay long. I…" Deep, deep breath. "I have to get home. To Jennie."

"To who?"

"Her name is Jennie," Travis said quietly. "And I guess it's time you guys knew about her."

Jake finally located his tongue, hanging somewhere in the vicinity of his chest.

"Sounds good," he said.

Then he hung up the phone, called Caleb and said, "You are never going to believe this but it looks like Travis is hooked."

"Hooked?"

"As in, he's coming by tonight."

"So?"

"He won't stay long. He has a woman waiting for him. At home."

There was a moment of silence. Then Caleb Wilde laughed.

"Uh-oh," he said.

Jake grinned. "Ain't that the truth?"

* * *

A few hours later, Travis paced the living room of his penthouse.

He'd gone home early.

Stupid thing to do.

Today was Jennie's late day at the university. She wouldn't be home for another half hour, which was more than enough time for him to have second-guessed himself a hundred times.

Telling Jake he'd meet him and Caleb tonight. What for? He was going to tell Jennie he loved her. He wouldn't want to leave her after that.

Okay.

Okay, no problem.

He'd take her with him. Introduce her to his brothers…

No. Forget that. He'd tell her he loved her. Then she'd tell him what it was that, when he least expected it, stole the joy from her smile.

Travis ran his hands through his hair.

Dumb thing to do, piling on so many heavy things for one eve—

The elevator hummed. Made the soft thump it always made when it stopped.

He swung toward it.

The doors opened.

Jennie stepped from the car.

"Sweetheart," he said…

And stopped.

God, the look on her face! It was one of such sorrow that he forgot everything, ran to her, took her in his arms and drew her into the room.

"Jen? What's wrong?"

"Nothing."

She was lying. He could see it. He could feel it, too. She was trembling.

He scooped her up. Carried her to a big leather chair. Sat down with her held tightly in his arms.

"Honey. Don't lock me out. I know there's something you're keeping from me—"

"I love you," she said. "I know I'm not supposed to tell you that but—"

He could have sworn he felt his heart take wing.

"Jennie. My beloved Jennie. I love you, too."

"See, I've studied the dynamics of—of—" For an instant, her eyes lit with happiness. "What did you say?"

"I said I adore you. I love you. I want to marry you. I want us to have kids, raise horses, do whatever makes you happy as we grow old together…"

A sob burst from her throat.

"No! I can't."

"Jennie—"

She shot to her feet.

"I can't marry you," she whispered.

"Of course you can."

She shook her head. "No. You don't understand. There's something I—something I haven't told you. I should have. I know I should have, but—"

Travis stood and gathered her into his arms.

"Whatever it is," he said softly, "we'll deal with it."

She made a little sound, something between a laugh and a sob.

"We can't deal with it."

"Of course we can. *I* can. Is it a legal problem? Caleb will help us. Is it something in your past? Whatever it is—"

"I'm sick."

"I know. The migraines. We'll take care of those, too. My doctor—"

"Travis." Jennie took a deep breath. Travis tried to draw her closer to him, but she kept a distance between them by flattening her hands against his chest. "I—I have—I have…"

She shut her eyes, then opened them again, and looked into the eyes of her lover. "I have a tumor," she whispered. "In my brain."

He stared at her while he tried to process her words.

"A tumor? But—"

"In my brain. And there is no 'but.' It's been there for months, and it's been growing." She drew a shallow, sharp breath. "My symptoms—"

"The headaches," he said hoarsely.

She nodded.

"Travis. I'm—I'm dying."

The room tilted. He thought he was going to pass out but he couldn't, he had to be strong for his Jennie.

Besides, it couldn't be true. He told her that she must have been misdiagnosed.

She got her briefcase. She had a file in it. Reports, scan results.

The diagnosis was accurate.

He told her how foolish it was to rely on tests from one hospital.

She spread the reports over the dining room table.

The tests had been repeated in three different major medical centers.

He stared at the papers. An icy hand seemed to close around his heart.

"Why didn't you tell me?" he finally said.

"I should have. I should have let you know the truth so that you wouldn't—you wouldn't have become involved with—"

He grabbed her. Silenced her with a kiss that tasted of terror and panic and desperation.

"I love you," he said. "I love you! Do you think knowing this—this thing is inside your head would have kept me from loving you?"

She wept.

He wanted to weep with her, but his brain was whirring. He needed a plan.

Minutes later, he had one.

"I know people in Germany. In the U.K. Hell, I know people all over the world. We'll fly to Europe—"

"Travis. My beloved Travis." Her voice broke as she looked up into his eyes. "It's all over. I've just come from my doctor. He says—"

Travis slammed his fist against the table.

"I don't give a good goddamn what your doctor says! I'm not going to let this happen. I refuse to let it happen. I love you, love you, love you—"

She rose on her toes. Kissed him. Kissed him again and again, until he responded.

"Make love to me," she pleaded. "Now. Make love to me—"

He took her there, in the living room, with passion, with tenderness, giving her all that he was.

She gave him all that she was in return.

At the end, she cried. And fell asleep in his arms.

He held her tightly to him, felt the beating of her heart, the warmth of her breath.

"I will not let you die," he said, his voice low and hard and fierce with determination. "I—will—not—let—it—happen!"

Finally, exhausted, he slept…

And dreamed.

Jennie was standing next to him. Leaning over him.

She was weeping.

"Goodbye, my love," she whispered, "goodbye."

Her lips brushed his forehead.

He stirred. Came awake…

And found himself alone.

"Jennie?" he said.

He went from room to room. There was no sign of her.

Panic beat leathery wings in his chest.

He called her on her cell phone.

She didn't answer.

He ran for his car. Drove to her apartment.

She wasn't there.

He checked her office on campus.

Nothing.

God, dear God, where was she?

He went back to his place, driving like a madman in case she'd somehow materialized somewhere in those empty rooms, but she hadn't.

Where could she have gone? Who would possibly know? That woman at the bar that night. Edna? Barbara? Brenda. That was it, but how in hell could he find a woman named Brenda in a city the size of Dallas?

"Think," he said aloud, "think!"

There had to be someone who'd know what she would do, where she would go...

Her doctor.

He would know.

But who was he? Where was his office? Dammit to hell, why didn't he have that information?

Maybe she had an address book. An appointment calendar. If she did, maybe the doctor's name and address would be in it.

Travis went through Jennie's things. Tore her stuff apart. Found no address book or appointment book or anything else.

Wait a minute. Would the medicines she took have the doctor's name on the bottles?

He knew where she kept the tablets. Some were in a little silver pill box she carried in her purse. The rest were in his medicine cabinet.

Yes. There they were, but the only thing on the labels were the unpronounceable names of the meds, and the name and phone number of the pharmacy that had filled the prescriptions.

There were a frightening number of prescriptions.

He phoned the pharmacy. Spoke his way up the chain of command but nobody would tell him the doctor's name or anything beyond the fact that the law protected a patient's privacy.

There had to be a way…

Travis pumped his fist in the air.

There was. His pal. Ben Steinberg. Surely he could get the name of Jennie's guy out of the pharmacy staff.

He thought about phoning, decided against it, got in his car and raced to Ben's office, caught him just as he was leaving.

"Ben. I have to see you."

"Travis? Are you sick?"

"No. My friend is sick. My friend…" Travis swallowed hard. "The woman I love gets these terrible headaches…"

"Ah." Ben smiled. "Well, tell her to phone my office and—"

"You don't understand."

Ben looked at him. "Man," he said quietly, "you look like hell." He hesitated. "Okay. Come into my office and fill me in."

Travis did.

When he finished, Ben's expression was grave.

"Did she say what kind of brain tumor it is?"

Travis shook his head.

"All she'd tell me was that she was—that she was—"

Ben nodded. "Yeah. Okay. You need to find her but I don't see what I—"

"If I find her doctor, maybe he can tell me where she's gone." Travis reached in his pocket, took out a vial of tablets, handed them to his friend. "I called her pharmacy. They won't give me the doctor's name. But they'll give it to you."

Ben nodded again. He thought about ethics, and patient confidentiality, and the fact that a woman named Jennifer Cooper had made it clear she didn't want the man who loved her to be with her as she died.

Mostly, though, he thought about the fear, the desperation in the eyes of an old friend.

Then he reached for the phone.

CHAPTER ELEVEN

IN THE END, finding Jennie's doctor didn't help.

Peter Kipling didn't know where she'd gone, either.

"I wouldn't break patient confidentiality if I actually knew," he said, "but I'd at least tell you she was safe."

But she wasn't safe.

His Jennie was desperate and alone, probably in excruciating pain, with a death sentence hanging over her.

Hours later, an exhausted Travis finally stumbled into the bar where he was supposed to have paid a pleasant visit to his brothers.

They saw him come through the door, signaled him to their booth…and turned grim-faced when they got a closer look at him. His face was gray, his hair was standing up in little tufts.

He looked like he'd aged a dozen years.

"What's happened?" Jake said sharply.

Travis looked at them.

"Are you sick?"

"No. I'm not sick. It's my Jennie who's sick."

His brothers exchanged looks. *His Jennie?*

"She's missing." Travis sank into the booth. "I've been looking for her for hours but I can't find her."

Caleb and Jake exchanged another look.

A lover's quarrel? Something more serious?

"Listen," Jake said slowly, "if she doesn't want to see you—"

"She's gone, Jacob. She's vanished."

"What do you mean, vanished?"

"Vanished," Travis said wearily. He put his elbows on the table, rubbed his hand over his eyes. "I can't find her anywhere."

Caleb's jaw tightened. "I have contacts," he said. "The police. Some private guys I'd trust with my—"

"You don't understand."

"No," Jake said gently, "we don't. How about explaining?"

Travis grabbed the beer bottle that stood in front of Jake. He took a long, thirsty swallow. Then he put it down, looked from the concerned face of one brother to the equally concerned face of the other, and did exactly that.

It took ten long minutes.

When he'd finished, his brothers were silent. It was the kind of silence that means nobody can think of anything useful to say.

Finally, Caleb cleared his throat.

"Telling you we're sorry won't cut it."

Jake nodded in agreement. "What we need is to do something that will help you. And your girl."

"Jennie," Travis said. "Her name is Jennie."

"Jennie. Of course." Caleb rubbed his forehead. "I need her full name. Her cell phone number. Her address. The department she's in at the university."

Travis shook his head.

"I told you," he said, his voice hoarse with exhaustion, "she's turned off her phone. She isn't at her apartment. I checked her office on campus. She's gone."

"I understand," Caleb said carefully. "Still, give me the info. Everything you know about her. Places she likes. People she knows. Where she's from."

"Yeah. Okay." Travis gave a sharp, sad laugh. "It's something to do, anyway."

Caleb took a small notebook and a pen from his pocket, shoved them both toward Travis.

"I want the name of her doctor. His phone numbers. And Ben's number. I haven't spoken to him in years."

Travis nodded as he jotted down the things Caleb had requested.

"Trav?"

Travis looked at Jake.

"When I was hospitalized in D.C., you know, after I was wounded...I got to know some of the other patients. One was this Special Forces guy. He had a—he had a brain tumor."

"Jennie's is inoperable. The tests—"

"Yeah. So was his." Jake paused. "But there was this neurosurgeon...His family brought him in as a consultant. The next week, they moved the Special Forces dude out of Walter Reed. I don't know where they took him, but a couple of months later, there he was, stopping by for a visit, and he looked like a new man."

"Jake. What's this have to do with—"

"Maybe nothing. Maybe everything. I have the guy's number. Why don't I give him a call?"

"Holden says the neurologist treating Jennie is the best in Dallas."

"I'm going to give my friend a call anyway, okay?"

Travis nodded. "Sure," he said, but his eyes were dull with discouragement.

Another silence. Then Caleb slapped the table top and rose to his feet.

"Okay. Let's get started."

Jake rose, too. So did Travis. He looked from one of his brothers to the other.

"I feel so useless..." His voice broke. "There must be something I can do."

"There is," Jake said briskly. "Go home. Eat something. Get some sleep. You need to stay strong, for Jennie. And stay put, just in case she comes looking for you."

"Hell. You're right. I never thought of…" He took a long breath, then exhaled it. "Call me. Both of you. Even if it's only to tell me you haven't come up with anything, okay? Just—just keep in touch."

The brothers embraced.

"Don't give up hope," Caleb said softly.

"Caleb's right," Jake said. "This is a long way from over."

"Yeah," Travis said, but they all knew he was lying.

It took Caleb less than two hours to find Jennie through his network of contacts.

He phoned Jake with the news as he drove to Travis's condo.

"She's on a flight to Boston, where she'll change planes for Manchester, New Hampshire."

"Excellent," Jake replied. "That'll put her within spitting distance of Boston Memorial."

"What's Boston Memorial?"

"A major hospital—and the place where that Special Forces guy tells me the world's most prominent neurosurgeon is running a hush-hush experimental program."

"Why do those words scare the crap out of me? Hush-hush. Experimental." Caleb, who was driving far too fast, swerved around a truck. "Even that phrase, 'the world's most prominent neurosurgeon…' According to who?"

"According to whom," Jake said, automatically correcting his brother's grammar which was, Caleb know, a really good sign that Jake was feeling upbeat, even hopeful. "According to my guy, and I believe him."

"Okay. But if it's so secretive, if it's experimental, how do we get Jennie into the program? There's no time to waste, Jacob. We all know that."

"She's already in," Jake said. "My guy called the Boston neurosurgeon, faxed him her medical file. He phoned me." Jake gave a little laugh. "Turns out, there are times it pays to be a wounded warrior with a shiny medal."

Caleb nodded, as if Jake could see him. He knew how his brother hated to talk about what had happened to him during the war, how he shunned all publicity about the medal he'd won. That he'd shared such a thing with a stranger, used it for leverage, was filled with meaning.

"Good job, man," he said softly.

Jake cleared his throat. "Hey, it's for Travis, right? And there are no guarantees."

"You mean," Caleb said, "anything could happen."

"I mean," Jake said bluntly, "that first the surgeon has to check Jennie out and agree to do the operation. And even then—"

"Right." Caleb hesitated. "Travis will have to know that."

"He'll know it. And he'll go for it. Hell, man, it's all we've got."

"Sure. But will she?"

"Good question," Jake said. "Only one way to find out."

"I'm on my way to Travis's place right now," Caleb said.

"Me, too. Meet you there in ten."

"In five."

Jake made a sound that approximated a laugh.

Maybe, just maybe, things were looking up.

They arrived at Travis's condo less than a minute apart.

They'd told him to shower. Eat. Rest. The only certainty was that he'd showered: his hair was still wet, and he'd changed his clothes.

Aside from that, he looked like a man who'd been pacing the floor and slowly going crazy.

The way he greeted them confirmed it.

"I cannot go on doing this," he said. "Just standing around here, my thumb up my—"

"Calm down."

"Calm down?" He spun toward Jake, eyes blazing. "The woman I love is out there alone, a—a monster consuming her brain, and the best you can do is tell me to—"

"I have one of the Wilde jets standing by."

Travis blinked. He looked at Caleb.

"You found her? How? Where? Is she okay? Did she ask for me?"

"One question at a time, Trav. I pulled some strings. Called in some favors. She's okay, she's on a plane heading for Boston, and she couldn't ask for you because she doesn't know we found her."

"Boston," Travis said. "She's going home. To New England." His face twisted. "Doesn't she know I'd want to be with her?"

Jake and Caleb glanced at each other in unspoken agreement that there was no sense in trying to answer that question.

Obviously Travis knew it, too.

"Okay," he said, "let's go after her. She's from New Hampshire. How will she get there? Has she rented a car?"

"She's changing planes in Boston. Actually she has two changes—"

"Which gives us time to get to Boston before she does."

Jake and Caleb looked at each other.

Travis's voice was stronger. He was taking command. It gave them hope he'd come through this, no matter how it ended.

"I love her," he said, his voice filled with certainty. "I won't let her face this alone."

"Yeah." Caleb laid his hand on Travis's shoulder. "There's something else."

"What?"

Jake cleared his throat.

"It's a long story," he said, "but it turns out there's an experimental program. A surgery to treat—what the hell do you call these things? Inoperable meningiomas."

"An oxymoron," Travis said angrily. "If the thing is inoperable, there can't be a surgery for it."

"I'm not a doctor, okay? Maybe I'm saying it wrong but the guy I knew at Walter Reed…I told you, it's a long story. The bottom line is that there's a surgeon—a team—doing this stuff."

The hope that suddenly glowed in Travis's eyes made both his brothers want to take him in their arms.

They didn't.

They knew Travis had to stay focused. And strong.

"First, they'd have to agree Jennie qualifies for the operation. And then," Jake said with brutal frankness, "it doesn't always work. Some patients die during the procedure. Some never come out of the anesthesia and end up on life support. Some survive but they're—they're damaged."

Travis gave a bitter laugh. "That's your good news?"

"What I said was, it doesn't always work. But when it does…" Jake drew a breath. "When it does, those patients resume normal lives."

"Oh, God," Travis whispered. "Oh God, Jennie…"

"Don't get your hopes too high," Caleb said bluntly. "This is one huge risk. Jennie will have to understand that."

"You don't know her. My Jennie never met a risk she wouldn't take." He glanced at his watch. "Why are we still standing here? We're wasting time."

Jake and Caleb nodded. They could hear the courage, the energy in their brother's voice.

"Go on," Jake said. "Pack while we get things going. Then we'll get the hell out of here."

Travis nodded, headed for his bedroom.

Jake and Caleb would buy what they needed in Boston.

Both men phoned their wives, offered quick explanations of what was going down.

"Tell Travis I love him," Jake's wife said.

"Tell Travis we're all with him," Caleb's wife said.

Two minutes later, the Wildes were on their way to the airport.

They reached Boston an hour before Jennie's plane was due, and stood at the gate, waiting.

Travis had never imagined time could move so slowly.

Whenever he looked at his watch, the hands were in the same place on the dial.

After the fifth or sixth time, he figured it was broken—except, Jake's watch read the same as his.

Jake said, "How about coffee?"

Caleb said, "How about a sandwich?"

Travis shook his head. All he wanted, all he needed, was to see Jennie.

They waited. And waited.

At last, a plane taxied to the gate. A disembodied voice announced the arrival of the flight Jennie had taken.

The ramp door opened.

The first of the disembarking passengers appeared. Most of them hurried into the terminal.

After that, nothing.

Travis's heart was racing.

Where was she? Was Caleb's information wrong?

His breath caught.

There she was.

Walking slowly, her face white, her eyes huge. He could almost feel the pain throbbing in her head.

He wanted to run to her, sweep her into his arms...

She saw him.

And froze.

He had not let himself think about this. About how she would react on seeing him. She had left him, after all.

"Jennie," he said, and opened his arms.

She sobbed his name, and flew into them.

He held her to his heart. Rocked her in his embrace. She lifted her face to his and he kissed her, kissed her again and again.

She was weeping. He was, too.

Behind them, Jacob and Caleb looked at each other, then turned away.

Their eyes were damp.

It was turning into one hell of a day.

Jake had taken a suite at a hotel in Boston.

Caleb had arranged for a limo.

They drove to the hotel in silence after a brief conversation, Travis saying, "Honey, these are my brothers, Jacob and Caleb," Jennie saying, "Hi," Jake and Caleb saying *Hi* in return.

Then she'd looked at Travis and asked him why his brothers were with him, how had he found her and where were they going?

Travis had considered everything he had to tell her.

Yes, but not here.

Instead, he'd drawn her closer to him—he hadn't let go of her since she'd gone into his arms—kissed her temple and said, "Will you trust me, sweetheart?"

Jennie knew there was only one possible answer, and she'd given it.

"Yes," she'd whispered, because what else could she tell the man she had already trusted with her heart?

The suite was spacious. A sitting room. Three bedrooms. Three bathrooms.

Caleb and Jake vanished into two of the bedrooms.

Travis led Jennie into the third.

She was wobbling. Her eyes glittered. He knew it was with pain.

He sat her down on the edge of the bed. Knelt and slipped off her shoes.

"Do you want to sleep for a while, honey?" he said softly.

She shook her head, winced when she did.

"No. I want you to tell me what's going on. Your brothers are with you. Why? And why are all of you behaving like you have a big secret?"

He sat down next to her and clasped her hand.

"I refuse to let you die," he said in a low, fierce voice.

"Travis. I know you want to deny the truth. For a long time so did I. But—"

He silenced her with a tender kiss.

"Listen to me, just for a minute. Will do you that?"

Jennie sighed. "Okay," she whispered, "but—"

"I tried to find you," he said. "When I couldn't, I turned to my brothers for help. Caleb located you." He smiled. "Sometimes, it's useful to have a former spy in the family. Jake—Jake did other things."

Her eyes searched his. "What other things?"

"Remember, I told you he'd been wounded in Afghanistan. Badly wounded. He was hospitalized at Walter Reed, and while he was there, he met somebody, another soldier who—who had a tumor. Inoperable, like yours. At least, they said it was inoperable."

Jennie tore her hand from his and got to her feet.

"No," she said. "No more! I've tried a dozen cures. Nothing worked." Her voice broke. "I can't do it again, Travis. Believing there's—there's some kind of—of medical miracle, only to find out that—that…"

Travis rose and stood before her.

"Jake's friend was accepted into an experimental program, right here at Boston Memorial."

Jennie turned away and clapped her hands over her ears. "I'm not listening!"

"Honey. Please. Hear me out."

"I've done it all. Tests. Shots. Drugs and more drugs. I've seen a thousand doctors. All of it led to one thing." She swung toward him, her mouth trembling. "I'm dying, Travis. It's why I did all those—those crazy things. Why I wanted to experience as much of life as I could. I knew, sooner or later, I'd have to accept what was coming."

"Jennie—"

"And I did. I accepted it. Until I fell in love with you."

She'd said the only words he'd ever wanted to hear.

"Leaving you was the hardest thing I ever did." Her eyes searched his for understanding. "I love you so much—"

"Then why did you run away from me?"

"Because I love you! Because I didn't want you to be there to see—to see what's going to happen to me. Because I didn't want you to look back years from now and—and remember me broken and lost and drained of life—"

Travis pulled her into his arms and kissed her.

"What gives you the right to make those decisions for me?" he said gruffly. "I *love* you, dammit! I adore you. I want to be with you whatever happens."

"Even to see me die?"

"Even that," he said, his voice breaking. "But you won't. I'm trying to tell you about this surgery—"

"No."

"Jennie. Don't say 'no' until you hear me out."

"How about *you* hearing *me* out?" She stood straight within his embrace, her eyes locked to his. "I've done everything they told me to do, everything they said would work. Nothing did. Nothing will. And—and I can't go through it again. The hope. The desperate, awful hope and then the letdown." She took a breath. "It's over. I'm dying and there's no way to stop it—unless you believe in miracles and I have to tell you, I don't."

Travis framed her face with his hands.

"What I believe in," he said, "is you. Your strength. Your courage. Your determination. Add in some damned good science, a surgeon who's found a way to save lives. Would you walk away from that?"

"It's useless, don't you see? Useless!"

"I thought you were the girl who believed in taking risks."

Tears were flowing down Jennie's face.

"You're not fighting fair."

"No. I'm not. Why would I, when it comes to wanting you with me forever?"

"You're merciless," she said, but her eyes, her voice, said otherwise.

Travis forced a smile.

"That's me. The merciless Travis Wilde. A man who won't give up his woman without a fight." He stroked his hand down her back. "I'll be there. With you. I'll be at your side the whole time. My love, my heart, all that I am will be with you."

Jennie bit her lip.

"Suppose—suppose I said yes. Do you know the odds of me coming through something experimental?"

"When we meet the surgeon, he'll tell us."

"And—and if I didn't come through, if I didn't survive, I wouldn't know the difference. But you would. I know you, Travis. You'd eat yourself alive for having had even the smallest part in this."

"I'll eat myself alive if I just let you leave me." His eyes darkened. "Fight for your life, honey. I'll fight for it with you. The doctors will do their part. We'll do ours. Just don't give up. I need you to be the girl who loves roller coasters, because that's the girl you really are."

Jennie didn't answer. He wondered if she'd really heard him, if she understood how much he adored her.

At long last, she laid her head against his shoulder.

"All right," she said quietly. "I'll meet with the surgeon."

Travis started to speak. She put her hand over his lips.

"I'll talk with him, but I can't promise more than that."

"Okay. That's good. It's fine. We'll talk to him."

"We?"

"Yes. Because we're one unit, honey. I'm you. You're me. Unless, of course, you don't want me to—"

She kissed him.

"Take me to bed," she said softly.

"Honey. You're so pale. And I know your head hurts."

"Take me to bed," she said. "Just hold me." Her voice trembled. "I need to feel your body warm and hard against mine."

He took her to bed. And held her.

And when she turned toward him, kissed him, stroked him to life, he made tender love to her.

She fell asleep.

Then he rose, dressed, went quietly into the sitting room where his brothers were waiting.

"Make the appointment," he said. "To meet with the doctor."

Jake smiled. "Already done. Tomorrow morning at 8:00 a.m." He went to Travis and held out his hand. "She's one hell of a woman," he said, and Travis, not trusting himself to speak, nodded as he shook Jake's hand, then Caleb's.

They were right.

His Jennie was one hell of a woman.

And if he needed proof, which he surely didn't, he got it the next morning when he and Jennie met with the surgeon.

She answered dozens of questions clearly and calmly.

Underwent endless tests, some of which looked like they'd been dreamed up by aliens.

At noon, the surgeon met with them again.

"Okay," he said briskly, "as far as we're concerned, it's a go."

Travis squeezed Jennie's hand.

"The odds on my making it through the operation?" she said.

"Fifty-fifty."

Travis winced but Jennie nodded.

"Thank you for being honest."

"No sense in anything else, Ms. Cooper. It's important you know as much of the truth as I know."

"And what about coming through but—but being a vegetable? What are the odds on that?"

"Honey," Travis said.

Jennie shushed him.

"I need to know," she said, "because I think I'm even more afraid of that than I am of dying. Doctor? What odds will you give me?"

"Better ones. Better, in your favor." The doctor smiled; then his smile faded. "But it's always a possibility."

Silence.

Jennie's face revealed nothing.

Travis, who had pushed her to get this far, hated himself for it. A fifty-fifty chance she would die. A slightly lower chance she'd survive with severe brain damage.

"No," he heard himself say. "No, honey, you can't—"

Jennie reached for his hand.

"When's the soonest we can do this?" she said. "Because now that I've decided to do it, I really don't want to sit around and wait."

"Actually," the doctor said gently, "we can't afford to wait. How does tomorrow morning at 6:00 a.m. sound, Jennie?"

Travis felt like a man standing at the edge of an abyss.

"Wait. We need to—to talk. Do some research—"

Jennie looked at him. "I want to do this," she said calmly. "And I need you to be strong for me."

She was right. They both had to be strong. And, suddenly, he knew exactly how they would get that strength.

"Marry me," he said.

Jennie's smile trembled. "If I can, when this is over—"

"Not then. Marry me now. Tonight."

"No. No! What if—"

"I love you," Travis said. "I'll always love you." He took her in his arms. "When you go into that operating room tomorrow, you're going in there as my wife."

Jennie cried. She laughed. She kissed the man she loved.

"Do I get a say in this, Mr. Wilde?"

"No. You don't." His eyes took on a suspicious glitter. "Get on the roller coaster, honey," he whispered. "Take this ride with me."

She kissed him.

And she said, "Yes."

CHAPTER TWELVE

AT FIVE MINUTES of eight that evening, the Wilde brothers gathered in the hospital's Serenity chapel.

It was a glass-walled room with a small fountain as its focal point. Water from the fountain ran over shiny black and gray stones, creating a peaceful sound. Slender ornamental trees provided a soothing touch of green.

Caleb and Jacob had been busy.

Caleb had come up with another old "contact" who'd located a judge powerful enough to arrange the waiver of the usual license requirements and to perform the ceremony.

Jake had somehow found a florist who'd miraculously arranged for dozens of white roses and white orchids to be delivered to the chapel in record time.

Travis wanted to tell his brothers what their thoughtfulness meant to him but he didn't trust himself to speak.

He didn't have to.

His brothers hugged him and made it clear they understood.

Promptly at eight, the chapel doors opened.

Jennie appeared, on the arm of her surgeon.

He wore a dark suit.

She wore a short white lace dress, courtesy of one the nurses who was part of the team that would be taking care of her. The dress was simple and beautiful.

As beautiful as the bride herself.

Travis stood straight and tall.

He smiled at her, and she smiled back.

And, in that instant, he knew he had been waiting for this woman, for this moment, his entire life.

Music began playing, an instrumental version of "And I Will Always Love You," courtesy of Jake's iPod.

Jennie's face lit.

Still on her doctor's arm, she started toward Travis. Her steps wobbled at the very end, and Travis stepped quickly forward and took her in his arms.

"I love you," he said softly, and she smiled again, her eyes glittering with happy tears.

The service was brief.

The judge spoke of love and commitment, joy and sorrow, of how love was life's one true constant.

When it was time to make their vows, Travis realized they didn't have rings...

Except, they did.

Jake and Caleb had thought of everything.

Jake handed him a plain gold band to put on Jennie's finger.

Caleb handed Jennie a matching band to put on Travis's finger.

It was time to speak their vows.

"I, Travis Wilde, take this woman, Jennifer Cooper..."

His voice was strong and sure.

Jennie looked into his eyes.

"I, Jennifer Cooper, take this man, Travis Wilde..."

She spoke softly, but her words were clear and certain.

A moment later, the judge smiled.

"By the rights vested in me by the State of Massachusetts," she said, "I now pronounce you husband and wife. Mr. Wilde—Travis—you may kiss your bride."

Travis cupped his wife's face in his big hands.

Both of them were smiling. Both of them had tears in their eyes.

"Mrs. Wilde," he said softly.

Jennie laughed. "Mr. Wilde."

"I love you," he said.

She put her arms around his neck. He lowered his head to hers.

And as they kissed, he knew that the words, *I love you,* could never be enough to tell her what she really meant to him.

Travis spent the night by his wife's side.

He'd brought her two wedding gifts.

Her beloved, one-eared plush dog, which he'd arranged to arrive by courier..

And a hand-written IOU, promising her a kitten.

She wept, kissed him, and they held each other close.

At a few minutes before six the next morning, the surgeon came by. He shook Travis's hand, gave Jennie a quick hug.

Moments later, an attendant wheeled Jennie from her room.

Travis went with the gurney as far as they'd let him, holding his wife's hand, smiling at her, telling her how much he adored her, that he'd see her very soon, that as she fell asleep, he wanted her to think about where she wanted to spend their honeymoon.

"New York," he said. "Or Paris or Rome, or anywhere you choose."

She was already a little groggy from medication; her voice was slurred but her words were deliberate.

"I want to go home," she said. "To your place in Dallas. That's home to me, it has been ever since we met."

"Right," he said brightly, "of course," he said, even more brightly because he was a heartbeat away from sobbing.

The gurney stopped.

There were massive doors ahead.

"Sorry, Mr. Wilde," one of the attendants said softly, "this is as far as you can go."

Travis bent over the gurney. He put his arms around Jennie as best he could and lifted her closer.

"Think of me," he whispered. "Think of us. Think about all the years ahead."

"I love you," she said. "I love you, love you, love you…"

The gurney started moving. The doors opened, then shut.

Travis stumbled back against the wall.

Long minutes later, he made his way slowly to the private waiting room the hospital had arranged for the Wildes.

His brothers were there.

"Trav," they said, and they drew him into their strong arms.

Time passed, but surely snails moved faster.

One minute. Two. An hour.

And, while the hands of the clock on the wall, the hands of the watch on Travis's wrist crawled forward, amazing things began to happen.

The door opened, and Emily and Jaimie walked into the waiting room.

Travis looked up, saw them and got to his feet.

"Travis," they said, and he opened his arms and they flew to him.

His sisters-in-law appeared a little while after that.

"Sage," he said hoarsely, "Addison…"

They kissed him, whispered words of encouragement.

God, he thought, *I am a lucky man!*

Lissa showed up next.

He knew she must have flown in from California on the red eye, that she probably hadn't slept, but her tear-shot smile and hugs were all a brother could ever want.

A couple of hours later, the door swung open again.

Travis rose slowly to his feet.

"Dad?"

General Wilde walked straight to his son.

"Travis," he said. He held out his hand. Travis reached for it but then his father cleared his throat, pulled back his hand and wrapped Travis in tight embrace.

"I got here as soon as I could."

Travis nodded. "I—I—"

"I hear your Jennie is quite a woman."

Travis tried to say yes, she was, but all that came out was a choked sound of joy.

Morning became afternoon, afternoon became evening.

Lights blazed on in the waiting room.

Darkness descended over the city.

The Wildes paced.

Talked in low voices.

Endlessly looked at the clock. At their watches.

Lissa, Sage and Emily left, came back with stacks of newspapers and magazines that went untouched.

Jaimie and Addison went out, returned with sandwiches, pastries and munchies.

Those went untouched, as well.

Jake disappeared, brought back a pizza.

Caleb vanished, showed up with two boxes of doughnuts.

"You have to eat," they all told Travis, but he didn't and neither did they.

Coffee, however, was a big success.

Everybody gulped it down.

After a while, by unspoken agreement, they stopped checking the time.

What was the point?

Time was either their friend—the surgery was taking so long because every step was going well—or it was their enemy—the surgery was taking so long because nothing about it was going well.

Every now and then, somebody in hospital green appeared in the doorway.

The first time, they all leaped to their feet, but it turned out the operating room team had simply sent someone to say that the surgery was progressing.

"How much longer?" Travis said.

He didn't get an answer.

The second time, he changed the question.

"How is my wife?" he asked.

The answer was still the same, but with an addendum.

The surgery was progressing, and the doctor would be down to see them when it was over.

Fourteen hours into what had become the longest day in the history of the universe, the neurosurgeon walked into the room.

He looked exhausted, and his expression was impossible to read.

The Wildes, almost as haggard-looking as he, sprang to their feet. Without plan or discussion, they gathered around Travis in a protective semicircle.

Travis opened his mouth, then shut it.

It was the general who finally spoke.

"My daughter-in-law?"

The surgeon nodded.

"She made it through," he said, his eyes on Travis.

Travis's knees buckled. Caleb and Jake, standing on either side of him, grasped him by the elbows.

"And?" Travis said hoarsely.

"The tumor's gone. We got it all."

Travis nodded.

"Is she…" He hesitated. "Is she all right? Was there any—was there any—"

"She's stable. Her vital signs are good. But…"

That "but" made all the Wildes stop breathing.

"But, we're not out of the woods until she regains consciousness."

Travis nodded again. It seemed all he was capable of doing.

"You mean, when the anesthesia wears off."

"She's unconscious, Travis. It isn't the anesthesia. It's her brain's reaction to the trauma of surgery." The doctor cleared his throat. "We just have to wait. I wish I could be more helpful but I can't."

Another nod.

"I understand," Travis said. He didn't, not really, but what was the sense in admitting it?

They had to wait. They just had to wait...

"I want to be with her."

"Travis," the doctor said, not unkindly, "the best thing you can do is go back to your hotel, eat something, get some sleep. We'll call you the second your wife—"

"I want to be with her," Travis said, in a tone that would not admit any argument.

The doctor sighed.

"She's in recovery. We'll let you know when she's in her room. You can see her then."

Two more hours dragged by.

Travis told everyone to go to the hotel.

"I'll phone," he said. "I promise."

"Not yet," Jaimie said softly, and the others echoed those words.

At last, a nurse appeared.

"Mrs. Wilde is in her room," she said. "Mr. Wilde, if you'd come with me..."

Travis rose slowly to his feet.

His brothers hugged him. His father patted his back. His sisters and sisters-in-law kissed him.

"I'll call you," he said.

And he followed the nurse out the door.

* * *

Jennie was sleeping.

He could almost believe that because of her peaceful expression.

But there were tubes everywhere. Her head was wrapped in layers and layers of gauze. She was hooked to a battery of machines.

"Sweetheart," Travis said.

"She can't hear you, Mr. Wilde," the nurse said gently.

Travis ignored her.

He drew a chair close to the bed, wrapped his hand around his wife's and said, "Baby, it's me. I'm here. And I love you."

The surgeon came by.

Checked the machines, the tubes. Gently lifted Jennie's eyelids, shone a light into her eyes.

"Well?" Travis said.

"Nothing's changed. And that's good. She's holding her own."

Travis nodded but it wasn't good. He wanted to hear that his wife was coming back to herself, back to him.

"You might want to get some sleep," the surgeon said. "In that lounge. Someone will wake you if—"

"I'm staying with my wife."

The doctor smiled.

"Of course."

The lights were bright.

A police siren was blaring.

Travis shot upright.

He'd fallen asleep bent forward, his head on the bed. It was daylight—that was the brightness in the room. And somewhere in the distance, a police car was racing toward its destination.

Jennie had not moved.

Travis could feel his cell phone vibrating.

He ignored it.

It stopped. Then it vibrated again.

He frowned, carefully let go of his wife's hand, got to his feet, took the phone from his pocket and walked to the windows.

Jake: "It's me, Trav. Anything?"

Travis shook his head, as if his brother could see him. "No."

Caleb: "What can we bring you? Some Danish? Bagels?"

"Nothing. Just—just wait at the hotel."

"Trav. You shouldn't be alone…"

"I'm not," Travis said gruffly. "I'm with my wife."

More time went by.

The Wilde bunch gathered in the private waiting room, same as the prior day.

Travis had no idea they were there.

They'd agreed they had to be there, for themselves if not for him, but they suspected that knowing they were there, worrying about them, would be a distraction that would not do him any good.

They spoke in hushed voices about everything, anything… and nothing, because they only topic on anyone's mind was Jennie Wilde and what the healing process would reveal.

Nobody wanted to take things further than that.

It was close to sundown.

Streetlights outside the hospital blinked on.

It was raining.

Inside the hospital, the corridor lights brightened.

Jennie still lay motionless with her husband seated beside her, clutching her hand.

He was talking to her, as he had been most of the last hours, babbling about whatever came into his head.

"Football season's coming," he said. "Do you like football? Did I ever tell you I played? I bet you'd be great at touch football. My brothers and I play sometime. My sisters, too, and Addison. Not Sage, 'cause she's pregnant. Did you know that? I'm going to be an uncle. Heck, you're going to be an aunt…"

His voice faded.

Jennie didn't move.

Despair was a wild thing, clawing for purchase in his chest.

"So," he said thickly, "are you one of those women who likes sports? No? Doesn't matter to me, sweetheart. I'll be happy for the chance to quarrel over the TV remote, you know, me clicking on a baseball game, you grabbing the remote and clicking on a couple of talking heads…"

Without warning, a sob broke from his throat.

"Jennie. Talk to me. Please, honey…"

He kissed her hand. Laid it gently on her chest. Got to his feet and walked to the window because he couldn't cry in front of her just in case she could hear or see or know or—

"…ice skate."

Travis spun around.

"Baby?"

"Always wanted to learn to ice skate," his Jennie said, her voice soft and fuzzy around the edges but, God, it was her voice, her voice…

He hurried to the bed. Wrapped his hand around hers.

"Jennie?"

Slowly, slowly, her lashes lifted.

"Jennie. Oh, God, Jennie!"

She turned her head. Her eyes were wide open, her gaze clear, her pupils focused directly on him.

"Travis?" She began to weep. "Is that really, really you?"

Travis sank onto the edge of the bed. Tears streamed down his face as he took his wife in his arms.

"It's me," he said. "I'm here, and so are you."

Her lips trembled, then curved in the most wonderful smile he had ever seen.

"Wasn't it a lovely wedding?" she whispered.

Travis laughed. He cried.

"It was perfect," he said.

He kissed her. She kissed him back.

Outside, the rain suddenly stopped, revealing the setting sun.

Soon, the moon would rise.

And the lives of Travis and Jennie Wilde would start all over again.

EPILOGUE

THE RESIDENTS OF Wilde's Crossing disagreed on lots of things.

Politics. Health care. The economy. Soybean futures.

Most of the arguing was genial, but it was still arguing.

People couldn't agree on everything…

Except on the party General John Hamilton Wilde threw a year later at *El Sueño*.

It was, they all said, the best party in the best town the state of Texas had ever seen.

A line of barbecue grills a mile long.

Well, maybe a slight exaggeration there but the point was, nobody could recall ever having seen so many grills in one place.

Tables groaning under the weight of salads and slaw, green beans and corn. Grits done a dozen different ways. Fried chicken. Biscuits. Cakes. Pies. Cookies.

More tables loaded with things to drink.

Punch. Wine. Beer. Ale. Good Texas whiskey. Coffee. Tea. Lemonade.

Nobody went thirsty.

A wooden dance floor had been laid behind the house. There was a band to play what Wilde's Crossing kids called oldies, another to play rock. There was a Mexican mariachi band. And inside the house, in the big, wood-paneled library, a string quartet played whatever it was that string quartets played, for the more sedate guests.

"Something for everyone," Travis said softly to his wife, as he held her in his arms behind a big cottonwood tree.

She smiled. His heart swelled. She had, without question, the most dazzling smile in the world.

"All I need is you," she said.

"I couldn't agree more," he said, smiling back at her.

She sighed. Laid her head against his shoulder.

"You have a wonderful family."

"It's your family, too, honey. And you're right. They're something special. Even the old man."

"Emily says he's changed."

Travis chuckled. "The understatement of the year."

"Well, look at all that's happened in that year," Jennie said. "Caleb and Sage had a baby."

"Uh-huh."

"Jake and Addison are pregnant."

"Right."

"And so are we."

"Exact…" Travis jerked back. "What?"

His wife laughed.

"We're having a baby," she said.

She watched the different emotions race through her husband's eyes. Shock. Joy. And, as she'd expected, a little touch of fear.

"It's fine," she said softly.

"You spoke with—"

"I called the doctor this morning. Yes. It's just the way he said, Travis. The tumor's completely gone. I'm okay. One hundred percent okay." She leaned back in his arms and smiled up at him. "So, we're pregnant. You're going to be a daddy."

Travis blinked.

"A daddy. I'm going to be a—"

He laughed. Whooped. Bent his beautiful wife back over his arm and kissed her breathless.

"I love you, Travis Wilde," she said against his lips.

"And I love you," he said. "With all my heart. And I always will."

Not terribly far away, within hearing distance but, thankfully, obscured by the branches of a giant oak, Emily, Lissa and Jaimie Wilde stood frozen in place.

They'd never intended to spy on their brother and sister-in-law; in fact, they hadn't even known Travis and Jennie were there.

They'd taken a stroll to get away from the party for a few minutes, to get away from, as Lissa had put it, "the busybody matchmakers."

"Every female over the age of twelve seems determined to marry us off," Emily had said, with a shudder.

"They seem to think it's time, now that the boys are married," Jaimie had agreed, with a matching shudder.

"Yeah," Lissa had said, "well, good for them. But I'm not looking for marriage."

"Not now," Em had said.

"Maybe not ever," Jaimie had added.

So, being trapped behind a tree, having to listen to their brother and his wife, had been, well, okay, it had been...

"Sweet," Lissa offered, as Travis and Jennie finally strolled away.

"We'll have to remember to look surprised when they announce that they're having a baby," Em pointed out.

"Definitely," Jaimie said. "And, really, I'm glad they're happy. All of them, you know? But—"

"But," Lissa said solemnly, "that isn't what I want."

"I don't, either."

"Same for me."

The sisters nodded. Then, because they were Wildes,

which meant they weren't just easy on the eyes, they were also smart, Em grinned and raised the bottle of Champagne she'd snatched for liquid sustenance from one of the party tables before they'd set off on their little walk.

Her sisters grinned, too. Lissa lifted her flute and Em's; Jaimie raised hers.

"To men," Em said, popping the Champagne cork with a flourish.

"Got to keep them where they belong," Lissa said, as Em filled the glasses.

"In bed. And around when you need something heavy lifted," Jaimie said.

"Aside from that," Em said, "give us the single life!"

The sisters laughed, cheered, slugged back the Champagne.

And thanked whatever gods might be watching for the freedom to be women, and not yet wives.

* * * * *

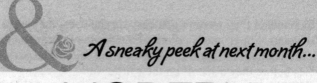

A sneaky peek at next month...

MODERN™

INTERNATIONAL AFFAIRS, SEDUCTION & PASSION GUARANTEED

My wish list for next month's titles...

In stores from 19th April 2013:

❏ A Rich Man's Whim — Lynne Graham

❏ A Touch of Notoriety — Carole Mortimer

❏ Maid for Montero — Kim Lawrence

❏ Captive in his Castle — Chantelle Shaw

❏ Heir to a Dark Inheritance — Maisey Yates

In stores from 3rd May 2013:

❏ A Price Worth Paying? — Trish Morey

❏ The Secret Casella Baby — Cathy Williams

❏ Strictly Temporary — Robyn Grady

❏ Her Deal with the Devil — Nicola Marsh

Available at WHSmith, Tesco, Asda, Eason, Amazon and Apple

Just can't wait?

 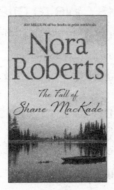